The Scottish Book of the Dead

a novel by

Gavin Broom

Island City Publishing LLC
Okemos, MI 48864

ISBN: 1-946890-08-1
ISBN-13: 978-1-946890-08-5

Dedicated to the memory.

May he grant unto the ka of Osiris Ani to behold the disk of the Sun and to see the Moon-god without ceasing, every day; and may my soul come forth and walk hither and thither and whithersoever it pleaseth.
—*The Egyptian Book of the Dead (translation)*

I didnae ken the cunt was deid.
—*Auld Harry from down the stairs*

The Book of Descent

THE STORK AND THE HOLE IN THE GROUND

1

Folk are fannies and they fuck things up.

Out of everything, this is the thought that pulses the strongest in my head. It's what sings the loudest. It flashes the brightest. Because out of everything that's happened over the last few days, this is probably the one realisation that has its claws in anything like the truth. It's the thought that forces my lips into a sorry smile while Auntie Helen steps to one side and tells me to come on in.

There's no going back.

In the living room of my father's pokey wee flat, there's a cube of notepaper sitting on a nest of tables next to his chair. On the sides of the cube, there's the logo of the company he worked for years ago. Under the logo, there's a phone number that has an old dialling code that's a digit too short by today's standards. The top page of the cube is covered with my father's handwriting, neat and precise in black ink, and it doesn't take much for me to jump to the conclusion that I'm looking at the last thing he wrote before he got carted off to the infirmary. The last thing he ever wrote.

Aye. Folk are fannies, right enough.

Auntie Helen's already back to work, scooting around

the place with a black bin bag dragging across the carpet at the back of her. The bag's like a massive conker, full and round and covered in jaggy angles. Uncle Raymond's in the kitchen, still dressed in his Tesco uniform, drinking tea from one of my father's mugs. His copy of The Sun spread across his chest with a headline that screams, EARTH MOVES FOR CENTRAL SCOTLAND. When he sees me, he grunts a greeting and ruffles the paper. He looks like shite and much older than I imagined him to be. Auntie Helen, on the other hand, is the same big ball of energy she always was and the years have been kinder to her. It's been a while, right enough. A lot of shitty water has flowed beneath a lot of burning bridges.

There's no getting round it. There's no going back.

"There's hundreds ae them, Adam," Auntie Helen says to me without looking up.

"Hundreds of what?"

"Hundreds ae them pads." She must have spied me clocking them.

"Aye?" I ask.

She picks up a hard-backed book entitled *Search For The Tomb of Osiris* and chucks it in the bag. "Hundreds. He must've nicked them before he got laid off. What he was doing hanging on tae them for all these years, Christ only knows."

"You chucked the rest out?"

"No, not yet. I'm trying tae dae the big things first." Now she looks up. "How come?"

I shrug and pick up the cube from the nest of tables. The scribbles on the top page are an equation, and although I don't know what it's for and I'm not able to work any of it out, I remember enough from school to recognise that it's calculus. Differential or integral, I'm not sure, but it's definitely calculus, and after half-a-dozen lines of working, the answer's underlined twice at the bottom of the page.

"x^2," I say.

"What's that?" Auntie Helen asks, suddenly huffy. She's moved over to the bookcase now and is consigning an entire shelf of Alastair McLeans and Ian Flemings and Wilbur Smiths into a fresh black plastic abyss; first editions for all she knows.

"x^2," I say again. I wiggle the cube of paper at her, the bottom half yawning open like an accordion. "It's the answer to his sum."

For the first time since I arrived, she stops. She stands still. The black bag falls to the floor, and she plants her hands on her hips. She blows a wee strand of hair out of her eyes and nods at me, and I see how shiny her head is with sweat, despite the chill that's in the flat. I wonder exactly how long she's been here, if maybe she hasn't been home yet.

"I know," she says. "I told ye. There's hundreds ae them wee pads. There's nae telling what ye might find when ye've been here for more than five seconds, Adam."

Although I have been home, I haven't slept for around thirty hours so I'm feeling pretty spaced out and jittery, and so I know she must be the same or worse. That in mind, I stay calm, ignore the barbed comment and keep a tight hold on my temper. Today's not the day for arguments. This doesn't stop a bit of a burn igniting in my jaw and my cheeks, but I keep it together. Folk are fannies, I remind myself, and I don't rise to the bait. I keep shtoom.

Now, the only noises left in the living room are the rustling coming from Auntie Helen's black bag, the ruffling of Uncle Raymond's paper and the loud tick-tock of the big clock on the wall above the mantel. I remember that clock from being a bairn in a different house, and its long spindly legs still remind me of a spider or one of those big scary beetles. It seems to know I'm watching it and the ticks get quieter.

Beneath the clock, on the mantle there's a row of ornaments all shaped like animals. Again, from other times and another place, I remember them all—the sly fox, the big friendly cow, the mischievous cat—but there's one I don't think I've ever seen. In the middle, there's a stork, made from metal rather than ceramic, stretching its long neck up like a snake, opening its beak as though it's swallowing a fish. The whole range of critters pretend not to see me. They listen to the clock and wait for something to happen.

The quiet starts to freak me out, so I switch on the TV to

fill the gaps left by our lack of things to say. I'm more than a wee bit surprised—and the headline from Uncle Raymond's paper suddenly makes sense—when it seems that the wee earthquake from last night is on the breakfast news. It's not a big item. I'm not even particularly convinced they're taking it seriously. But still, for a second or two, that's my old primary school on the TV. That doesn't happen every day.

None of us acknowledges it. We can all hear it—I'm pretty sure Auntie Helen is sneaking wee looks at it—but the silence in the living room holds. There's my old primary school, there's the Co-Op down near the canal, there's the massive tree outside the West Church that looks a bit more lopsided today than it did yesterday, there's a house across the road from the Health Centre with bits of its roof caved in, there's the streets we all walk down, there's folk we know, and it's on the TV right now. Still, nobody says a word. Still, the critters on the mantle wait.

So I keep my mouth shut and flick through the cube in my hands. Right enough, there's more equations, more numbers, more lines of working and although they all seem to be slightly different, the answer at the bottom, underlined twice, is always the same—x^2—and when I think that this may well be on a hundred of these wee notepads, and when I think of how seemingly insignificant things about the town have changed overnight, for the first time, it hits me. It takes a massive fucking run-up and skelps me right across my face.

My dad is dead and he's not coming back, and I'm twenty-six and I've no idea how I'm supposed to deal with any of this.

2

ust like everything these past few days, time's pretty mental. Minutes turn to hours and hours turn back to seconds, and I've no control over which way it goes.

Last night, up at the infirmary, while I sat and waited on the doc to fill out all her forms and certificates, it felt like me and Auntie Helen were stuck in that room for round about nine million years. Maybe even as many as ten. Honest to God, I've had fortnight holidays that've passed quicker. Maybe it's not all that surprising. Until this week, we hadn't seen each other for years—ten years, according to Auntie Helen—and we were both still in that place where it was all about manners and smiles and a united front just in case the old man pulled through and we had to start getting on with each other again. So we spoke. We comforted each other. We reminisced. She gently took the piss out of what she called my posh university accent. And while we probably both wished we'd had someone different with us, I think we helped.

On the other hand, going home in the wee hours, trying not to wake up Caroline in her condition, slinking into bed, staring at the inside of my eyelids for a bit and then leaving the house while she still slept to come here seemed to pass in a jiffy.

So what feels like hours probably takes less than thirty seconds, and I hear myself asking Auntie Helen if she's looking for a hand.

"Well, I've not touched the bathroom," she says. After a wee pause, she adds, "Or his bedroom." She whispers something to herself that I don't quite catch.

"Oh, right. Eh?"

"I said I'm not ready for that," she snaps. "I'm not ready for his room. Not yet."

I shrug. "Fair enough. I could—"

"Aye, you could make a start on the lavvy, that'd be grand."

"But I don't mind—"

"Either that, you could phone yer mother."

I scratch the back of my head for a second and then grab a black bag and trot off to the bathroom.

It's more of a shower-room than a bathroom, given that there's not a bath, but it's tidy enough and far better than I'd feared. It's a sandy colour, and he's even got wee stencils of camels going nose tae tail around the walls, giving the place a bit of a desert feel. I don't know why but it makes me smile and then, almost immediately, it makes me want to cry. I haven't cried yet and I have no plans to start now with two strangers in the next room. So I swallow that feeling down. I cough. I give myself a shake. I get on with it.

I'm clearing out one of the two medicine cabinets—both of which could pass for a chemist's storeroom—when the phone starts ringing in the living room. Maybe it's because I'm overtired but for a minute, hearing the shrill chirp through the bathroom door and seeing the carousel of camels on the wall makes me feel dead dizzy, and I get all anxious to be back at my own house and to see Caroline and make sure she's alright, and then I realise I don't know what time it is, and I couldn't really say for sure what day it is, but it feels like it might be a Tuesday or a Wednesday, and maybe Caroline's still asleep and I really, really want to see her and wake her up and hug her and kiss her and still the phone's ringing away in the living room and I can't hear anyone making a move to answer it and now it's starting to get on my fucking wick.

"Phone!" I shout, pointlessly because they must be able

to hear it better than I can, better than they can hear me.

Still, it keeps on ringing, and I decide that Auntie Helen must've moved outside to the front landing or something.

"For fuck's sake," I mutter. Then I yell, "Uncle Raymond! Can you get that, please?" I know he's just off the night shift, and his wee brother's just died, but surely he can toddle out of his grief from the kitchen to pick up a phone.

Apparently not. Apparently, that newspaper of his is weighing him down. The bathroom leads out on to the living room, and as soon as I open the door, the cold air hits me, and I see Auntie Helen and Uncle Raymond standing in the middle of the floor, staring at the ringing phone.

"Is no one going to answer that?" I ask.

But if they're good at ignoring the phone, they're Olympic-standard at ignoring me. Their heads don't budge an inch, their eyes stuck on the ringing hunk of plastic that sits on the nest of tables, right next to where the notepad used to live.

Then something happens that I think Auntie Helen knew was going to happen but felt powerless to stop.

—Beep!

The answer-machine picks up.

My father takes a deep breath that wavers a bit, probably because he's nervous and he hates these things, hates the sound of his own voice.

"—S-sorry I cannae come tae the phone, but if ye leave yer name and a wee message after the beep, I'll get right back tae ye just as soon as I can. Cheerio, then."

There's a few seconds of silence. I picture my father frantically trying to find a button that says RIGHT, THAT'S ME FINISHED NOW, but mostly I'm thinking that's my father's voice and that's the first I've heard it in ten years, and that's the only way I'll ever hear it again, and I find myself willing him on, praying that he susses it out, that he doesn't make a fanny of himself. Finally, he must either find the right button, or he just pummels every one until he gets lucky and there's a

—Click!

and then another

—Beep!

and then it's done.

Before the caller can leave a message, Auntie Helen finds her legs and she plucks the phone off the nest of tables, grabs the cord and fucking yanks it out of the wall. And with the wee white box that's turned cream with age raised up over her head, and with the cords and wires and the receiver dangling down like tentacles, she chucks the phone to the floor and stamps on it, sending splinters of snapped plastic skimming under the couch and all roads.

We all stare at the carcass of the answer-machine, and nobody says a word. I hold my breath until Auntie Helen coughs and wipes her brow and says to me, "Have ye phoned yer mother yet?"

"You know I haven't," I snap, a bit shocked, a bit dizzy again, a bit louder than I meant. "I've been tidying out the lavvy."

"Well, ye'll need tae call her from yer own house or from yer mobile," Auntie Helen says. "I think yer father's phone might well be fucked."

3

The bathroom feels even smaller after the telephone incident. Now, even the tiniest item looks like it's dripping with significance. In a ceramic saucer on top of one of the medicine cabinets there's a copper bracelet that I can't imagine doing anything at all for his arthritis. The Gillette aftershave that somehow reminds me of the last Christmas we ever spent as a family, before my mother left us and before I left him a couple of years later. A rank hairbrush that I remember from when I was growing up is there, missing prongs, still looking like it's been used to scrape up spider's legs. Seeing his name printed on a hundred different pill bottles gives me goosebumps like I'm reading it from a Nobel Prize or an Oscar. A copy of last week's *News of the World* sits at the side of the lavvy on the floor, and round the margin of the front page there's more of his scribblings, more equations, more x^2s.

I black bag the lot. Every last bit of it. I need to. I need to get it out of my fucking sight.

4

Outside on the landing, on the other side of the front door, there's so many black bags that the whole scene is starting to look like we've got some alien monster queen cutting around, laying her eggs all over the place. Despite myself, I can't help but think the alien monster queen might be Auntie Helen and these black eggs are her babies.

"I think we've just about reached the biggest number ae black bags ye can fit out here." It's Auntie Helen. She's snuck up behind me, so close I feel her breath on my neck. After I clamber back into my skin and have a mini-crisis about her reading my mind, she drops another egg to the clutch. The hook of a hanger pokes through like a beak, and then something clicks in my head.

"That's what calculus is all about," I say.

"That's what what's all about?"

"Calculus," I say, already wishing I'd kept my mouth shut. "That's what all those notes are about."

"He's been working out how many black bags he can fit in his front landing?" She doesn't get it.

"No, just generally. It's calculus. It's all about working out the maximum capacity of things." I scratch the side of my head. "Ken, like volume and limits and that? At least, that's what I think it's about."

Auntie Helen looks at me as though I'm speaking in tongues while the bag in my hand gets heavier and I wonder if she really doesn't get it or if she just wants me to think she doesn't get it.

Eventually, she says, "We'll need tae start getting some ae these off tae the cowp," and then she goes back inside.

5

Uncle Raymond doesn't say a word. He coughs a few times and hums for a wee bit at whatever's on the radio. Other than that, there's not a peep out of him, and he's happy just to point his ancient wee Fiesta towards the town dump. When we get there, we'll need to make sure that nobody lobs it into one of the skips, thinking it's part of all the other crap we're chucking out. I nearly smile.

According to Auntie Helen, he's just started a new job working nights and couldn't take any time off, so I didn't see Uncle Raymond up at the infirmary over the last few days. I came close to saying something to Caroline about how weird it was that he couldn't be bothered to visit his own brother in hospital, but the hypocrisy of something like that smacked me in the mouth before the words could come out.

The last time I saw him before today would've been at Auntie Helen's fortieth birthday, back when the whole me-and-my-mother-and-my-father deal was about on its last legs. If I've to think about the last time I actually had a conversation with him, I'd have to go back further than that, to where my reference points are less reliable and much thinner on the ground.

He always was a bit of a funny bugger. That's what my mother told me, although she'd say burger in a lame attempt to avoid swearing. My father never had a bad word to say about him. I remember that. My father talked quite highly of big brother Raymond. I couldn't have been more than twelve or thirteen at the time, so I didn't know if he was funny burger or not, or why my mother felt that way. All I knew was, he and Auntie Helen got me nice things for my Christmases and birthdays, and that's pretty much all a wee laddie cares about. Uncle Raymond was just part of the package that came with Auntie Helen. I used to love Auntie Helen when I was a bairn.

In amongst all this is the niggle that I've still got to phone my mother. I check my watch. Somehow it's not even ten o'clock. I can't remember if it's a seven or eight-hour difference between here and Los Angeles but either way, it's still the middle of the night over there. I require no more persuasion than that to push the snooze button on this chore and send it off to the back of the queue. One thing at a time.

We get to the dump, and with it being early on a weekday morning, it's just us, the council workers and a bunch of seagulls that look to be having problems staying in the air. Above us all, low grey clouds rush along, caught in the jet stream or something. On the ground, though, it's oddly calm. We stop at the barrier and Uncle Raymond rolls down his window.

"What've ye got?" the guy on the barrier asks. He's got a leathery face, all tanned and cracked, his fluorescent jacket so old that's it's faded back to plain yellow. He has a peer into the back seat like a customs official on a cross-channel ferry. Just like the boot, the back's all crammed with black bags.

"General rubbish," Uncle Raymond mutters.

My stomach lurches. My head seems to compress behind my eyes. There's a whistled pitch in my ears that goes flat and my hands go all clammy, and the only reason I can come up with for any of this happening—apart from the sleep deprivation and a growling belly—is hearing Uncle Raymond's voice has made me realise how out of the ordinary all this is. What am I doing? What am I doing here? Who are these people? What are my priorities? Where's Caroline got to?

What if she turns up at the flat while we're out? How will she handle the cold in her condition? How will she handle Auntie Helen in any condition?

"Take it tae number five," the council guy says.

The barrier's lifted and we trundle past all the recycling skips to skip number five which has a massive sign over it that says NON RECYCLEABLE WASTE ONLY. NO CARDBOARD. NO PLASTICS. NO WOOD. NO METAL.

I think about a lot of things while Uncle Raymond and I hurl the bags into number five. It's hard to put my finger on any of it or keep track of where these thoughts go. Mostly, though, I'm just thinking about how much this hurts. With every bag I'm chucking away, it hurts me. And when I watch the bags bounce their way down the sides of the empty skip, it hurts. And when I see the bags collecting at the bottom, that hurts too. And I think it's because instead of books and CDs and notepads and pens and hankies and expired medicine, it might as well be arms and legs and a head and a heart and there's nobody around to watch any of this disposal. It's just me, Uncle Raymond and the council guy with the leathery skin. There's no priest or whatever. There's no relatives. No comforting words. No tears. It's just three strangers who aren't speaking to each other while they ignore the sign telling them that what they're doing is wrong.

6

When we turn on to my father's street, there's a one-man welcoming committee waiting for us at the kerbside outside his flat. At first, I don't know who it is, but as we pull up, I sort of recognise the guy as my father's downstairs neighbour, a guy I met once or twice just before everything turned to shite. He's a good bit older than my father—mid-seventies probably—and he's sitting on the wall that runs round the drying green, dressed in a brown cardigan, shirt and tie, polished shoes, a head full of thick, white hair. He'd be quite the dapper chappie if it wasn't for that cardy. He gets up just as Uncle Raymond's pulling on the hand-brake.

"Aw, son," the old man says when I get out. "I barely recognised ye."

Uncle Raymond ambles round the car, footering with his keys.

The old man grabs my hand. "Ye'll no mind me, son. I'm Harry. I've lived down the stairs from yer da since he moved in."

"I remember you, Harry," I say. "We met a couple of times, a few years ago now, right enough. It's nice to see you again."

"I just missed ye on yer way oot, there. I've been meaning tae catch ye, so I've kept an eye oot for ye coming back. I hoped ye widnae be too long."

"Aye, we were..." We were what? Flinging his shite into a skip? Systematically removing all traces of him from his own home before the day's out? "...we had a bit of business to take care of."

Harry nods. "Aye, there's plenty ae business tae take care ae, so there is."

"Keeps us busy, I suppose."

"I suppose so, son," he says. "So tell me, how's the auld boy doing anyway?"

I fucking choke. My mouth falls open. Aw, Jesus. Aw, Jesus suffering fuck.

"He died, Harry. He passed away last night." My tongue feels like a drowned fish in my dry mouth. "I...I thought you'd know."

He's still holding on to my hand, his eyes misting up now. "I'm so sorry, son. Course, I kent he was in the hospital but... ach, I didnae ken the cunt was deid. I'm so sorry, Adam. So sorry, Raymond."

Harry's face drops, and he starts shaking his head. Uncle Raymond walks by and disappears into the block without a word or a nod.

"Aye," I say. I don't know how I'm meant to respond to condolences because any reaction feels as false as the next. I'm starting to think that the best way to answer it is to emulate Uncle Raymond, so I manage a sad smile and let the burning in my throat cool and ease for the umpteenth time today.

Harry finally lets go of my hand, wipes his eyes and looks up. "He's been a great friend tae me these past ten year. A great friend. I dinnae ken what I would've done withoot him some days. Put a smile on my face, so he did. And he was always talking aboot ye, Adam."

"Aye?" I hear myself ask. He was always talking about me? After ten years? Really?

"Oh, aye. He was proud ae ye, son. Dinnae think for a minute that he wasnae. He was proud ae his boy making something ae himself, going to university..."

Right enough, he would've known about that or heard about it from somebody—

"...proud ye were writing for the wee paper..."

—and I guess he would've seen my name on the byline for my many pointless stories about Gala Days and missing cats and failed planning applications—

"...and it's such a shame that he's no gonnae get tae see his grandson or granddaughter. He's no gonnae get tae see the wee yin." Harry's tears come in a fresh burst. He covers his face with one hand and waves weakly at me with the other while he shuffles away. "I need tae go, son," he sobs. "I'm awfy sorry aboot yer da."

—and with that, he disappears back into his flat, leaving me standing out on the street next to Uncle Raymond's old rustbucket, wondering just what the fuck that was all about.

7

If possible, the flat's much colder when I get back. Auntie Helen is taking a break from black-bagging everything that isn't nailed down and has made a cup of tea for herself and Uncle Raymond. The TV's back on, turned to the local news where the earthquake is the main item and not the cheap, light-hearted, throwaway piece that it was on the national. I'm already knocked off my stride from my conversation with Harry, and I find myself mentally stumbling when I try to work out if all that really happened in the wee hours of this morning, less than twelve hours ago. I'm still not a hundred percent sure what day it is.

"Harry from down the stairs?" I say. It comes out more of a question that I intended. "D'you know what he said to me?"

"Wheesht the now," Auntie Helen says. "They're talking about yon earthquake."

I do as I'm told. I shoosh and sit down on the leather pouffé in the corner of the living room. I'm supposed to be a journalist, so I try to listen to the report—my colleagues must be run ragged today—but it takes more concentration that I can muster to get my brain to focus. The commentary passes through me, leaving no trace that it was ever there because the only words I can hear right now are the ones uttered by auld Harry from down the stairs.

The image of some guy's lawn with a crack running down the middle of it is all I can take in. There must be thirty folk crammed into the back garden of a standard council house. There's pensioners, a few neds, the police, neighbours, and there's a guy—presumably the owner, probably around my age—with a massive grin on his face like he's won the lottery. His wife or girlfriend is next to him looking far less chirpy about the whole affair but still managing to look pretty. Between the two of them, there's a wee laddie who looks half-asleep, his head resting against his mother's hip.

—He's no gonnae get tae see his grandson or granddaughter. He's no gonnae get tae see the wee yin.

It takes me a few seconds to notice that even though it's daytime and even though they're all outside, the whole family has bed-hair and are dressed in their jammies. The reporter's pointing a mic towards them. He nods, nods some more and then crouches on to his hunkers to ask the laddie something. The laddie's too sheepish and shy and sleepy, though, and with his chin now pressed into his chest, he squirms behind his mum and when the camera pulls back to the adults' faces the man is practically hysterical with laughter. The mother, with her hair six ways to Sunday, looks shell-shocked and about one wrong word away from crying or killing someone or bursting into flames. I think of my own family, of Caroline, of my mother—who I still haven't phoned—and my father. I wish something different had happened last night. I wish these people weren't on the TV.

"That's Aitchison Drive, isn't it?" Auntie Helen asks.

Uncle Raymond hums an agreement.

"I dinnae ken him," she goes on, "but I've seen her in the Coapy getting her messages. She's usually done up a bit better than that, right enough, with that wee laddie ae theirs in tow. He cannae be more than three, that bairn. A wee mummy's boy if ever I've seen one."

—He's no gonnae get tae see the wee yin.

"Cannae remember her name, though. Hold on, her man's one ae Kenny McBride's cousins, is he not? Ocht, what's her name? You'll ken Kenny McBride."

NON RECYCLEABLE WASTE ONLY.

An electric shiver runs through me, shaking me alert, practically sending my foot shooting out in front of me.

"Adam. Ye listening?"

"Aye. Sorry," I say. "Kenny McBride. Aye, he's never out of the court pages. I don't know those people, though. I guess he does have a McBride look about him."

"For a supposed toaty wee earth tremor, that's some crack in their back green. I'd say that was a bit more serious than they're making out."

So rather than react to my response to her question, Auntie Helen has decided to call upon her enviable cache of earthquake-related facts and opinions. I'm vaguely aware of thinking something sarcastic and probably rather nasty about this wisdom, but whatever it is, it's never in any real danger of being said out loud, and I let it slip away, the only clue that the thought ever existed being a small smile in the corner of my lips. The smile, small as it is, freezes when my attention drifts to the stork ornament on the mantel above the fire that's now on its own. I wonder why it's been left. I wonder why all its pals have presumably been black-bagged.

The news makes way to the sport, which in turn moves into the weather. While the camp guy with the tan points to the coast and does an impression of the wind whooshing west to east through the central belt, Auntie Helen murmurs that she hopes we get a nice day for the funeral. With mention of something to do with my father, I spot a chance to steer us towards auld Harry, but before I can even take a breath never mind utter a word, she's already off.

"Talking ae the funeral," she says as she turns to me, "do ye ken when it's going tae be, Adam?"

There's ambiguity in the question. It's probably deliberate. And there's something else in her tone, something equally deliberate, that makes me think this is a trap. Is she asking me if I know because she can't remember if she's told me already, or is she asking me because she thinks it's my job to arrange it? While I'm assessing which assumption will cause the least damage, I shrug. I don't mean to. There's nothing in the shrug. There's no drama. There's nothing intentional or dismissive. It's just the kind of shrug that people sometimes do when they're thinking about something. But even before my shoulders have fully gone down, given the ambiguity and the tone of her question, I know I've sprung the trap.

"What's that supposed tae mean?" she growls.

Uncle Raymond wanders away to the kitchen.

"What?" I ask.

"What d'ye mean, what?" she asks, mimicking me. "This," she says, and she shrugs except I'm sure mine wasn't so elaborate and I definitely didn't have my bottom lip pouting out.

"Sorry, I was just trying to remember if it was something we'd already talked about. No offence."

"No. We've not talked about it. How can we talk about it when ye've not fucking arranged anything?"

Calm. "Aw, wait a wee minute, here. I'm not even sure it's my—"

"A wee minute? Ye've not had tae dae fuck all for him for the last ten year, Adam. The least ye can do now he's deid is get yer arse into gear and dae something for him now."

Still calm. "But that's exactly it. I thought Uncle Raymond might want—"

"Never you mind about yer Uncle Raymond. Yer Uncle Raymond did plenty for him. As did I, before ye mention it. Twice a week I was in here cleaning up the place, doing his washing. Don't you worry about us, son. You take a look at yerself. Ten year, Adam. Ten fucking year."

Fuck calm. "It's all coming out now." The volume of my voice rises to match hers. "Why don't you tell me how you really feel, Auntie Helen?"

"No wonder when ye cannae arrange a bloody piss-up in a brewery."

"Well, if you know I haven't arranged anything, why are you asking me?"

Her arms fly out. "Tae get ye tae fucking dae it!" she shouts. "Tae get ye tae act like ye really have lost yer father instead ae mumping about like ye've been given housework tae dae!"

"You think this is a stroll in the park of me? You think it's easy to deal with any of this?"

"I couldnae care less!" Veins in her neck bulge. "I couldnae care less how this has been for ye. And while I'm at it, I couldnae care less if ye ever find a window in yer schedule to phone that fucking mother of yours. But he was yer father. And he's deid. And he deserves some respect, and he needs a funeral, and you're his next ae kin and you need to make the fucking arrangements!"

"Well, shouting at each other and your passive aggression and your fucking aggressive aggression for that matter isn't helping!" I yell. "And if we start picking scabs we're going to be here for a while."

"Words ae wisdom from Oprah fucking Winfrey sitting there. I've not got anything tae be ashamed of, son."

"And I have?"

"Aye!" she screams and even when she stops, it sounds as though it's still echoing out. Quieter, but not by much, she says, "Aye, Adam. Ye have."

Somewhere in amongst all this, I think of the auld man down the stairs—auld Harry—and I think of him sitting in his living room with his TV switched off and his blinds partially closed as a mark of respect. I think of the state he got himself in, and I imagine him staring up at his ceiling and his big light that must be swaying about with the vibrations of me and Auntie Helen giving each other hell. I wonder what he must be thinking. Then I wonder why I'm not thinking of my father. Maybe it's just easier.

I'm staring at the carpet when I say, practically in a whisper, "It wasn't all my fault."

When I look at Auntie Helen, her cheeks are flushed, and she's panting like a big dog. Her breath condenses in the chill of the flat and bubbles of spit sit on her lip. She's leaning forward in her seat like she's about ready to pounce across the room to me. I become very conscious that I'm sitting on a pouffé and if she clatters into me, I'm going to end up on my back and probably crushed to death.

Her breathing calms. Her complexion cools. Her head drops into her hands.

"He left me just as much as I left him," I say.

The wall clock that looks like a spider or a beetle ticks away like it's concentrating on keeping count. Uncle Raymond, who had a dog in the fight he's just witnessed, ruffles the newspaper as though the kitchen is an isolation booth.

"Aye, I ken, son," she says. "I ken. You're right."

I let this sit for a moment before I say, "You too. I should be sorting this stuff out. It's only right."

In this new calm and agreeable atmosphere, part of me expects her to say something like there not being an immediate rush or that we can both sort it out together, or that Uncle Raymond would like to be involved. But she doesn't, and as I get up and walk out to the front landing and the restocked collection of bulging black bags, her head stays in her hands.

It's a different sort of cold in the front landing. It's a welcome cold. My face must be red raw like a well-skelped arse and out here I can just about feel my cheeks suck the chill right out of the air.

I fish my mobile out of my pocket. The display tells me I've missed eight calls and I freak out a bit because I've had the phone with me all day and not heard or felt a thing and worry that something's happened to Caroline. A few checks later and not one of the calls is from her. Every single one of the eight has come from the office. I curse my boss under my breath. I told him I was taking the rest of the week off to get things sorted, but it'll be this earthquake business. They'll all be running about like they're covering the rapture.

I stare at the phone, at the cutsey wallpaper of me and Caroline dressed in Hawaiian gear, at our cheesy smiles. The photo was taken last year at her mate's twenty-first, before Caroline was expecting, at a time when I can honestly say I hadn't thought of my father or Auntie Helen or Uncle Raymond for years. And although it's only been a couple of days, I've spent them thinking of little else, and not of Caroline, and not of the bairn.

—He's no gonnae get tae see the wee yin.

Normality feels so far away I might never see it again. This might become normal. This might already be normal.

"Fuck it," I say, maybe aloud, maybe to myself.

I push the call button. I don't call the office. I don't call the Coapy funeral directors. I don't call my mother. Instead, I need a taste of something more familiar, just for a minute.

In the end, though, it feels further away than ever, because I call home twice, and both times it's my own voice that greets me as I explain to myself that nobody can come to the phone at the moment, but if I leave my name and my number, I'll get back to me as soon as I can.

8

The overly sympathetic man who answers the Coapy's phone tells me they'll send someone to my house later tonight, round about seven o'clock. He apologises for every question he's about to ask, and then he apologises after asking it. He wants to know how my father died, even though he says it's not vital and that it won't hold anything up. He says they get a lot of hoax callers and they've found that by asking this kind of question, it puts the pranksters off for some reason. I can't imagine why anyone would fake an appointment with a funeral director but, if my occupation has taught me nothing else about the people of this town, it takes all sorts. And apparently, it takes all sorts of lunatics.

—Folk are fannies and they fuck things up.

I make every possible assurance that I'm not pulling anyone's chain and answer all the questions as best as I can. The date for the funeral is pencilled in for Monday.

When I relay this back to Auntie Helen, she initially looks like I've put her nose out of joint like she was expecting the business to take place at her house, but that impression disappears quickly and then she looks appeased.

"That's fine, son," she says. "There's no going back now."

9

The fun and games and random bursts of profanity while dismantling my father's living room furniture are put on hold while Auntie Helen announces that it's time to take a break for a wee bite of lunch. I could just about kiss her. My belly's been thinking my throat's been cut since I got up this morning and I feel as if my whole body's rattling. In truth, this didn't help my temper when Auntie Helen and I were yelling at each other, and it didn't help my nerves when I couldn't get a hold of Caroline. I'll feel better when I get something to eat, I tell myself. I'll feel more like myself.

Auntie Helen gives Uncle Raymond twenty quid and sends him to McDonald's. I have no idea why, but this makes me laugh. Again, the lack of food runs the risk of exaggerating my emotions, and I come close to hysterics, still completely unaware of why, but knowing that if Uncle Raymond comes back with a Happy Meal, I'll most likely piss myself.

Thankfully, he comes back with cheeseburgers, fries, and Cokes. The smell of the food totally makes me alert and a bit high.

"You look like death warmed up, Uncle Raymond," I tell him cheerfully, and it's true. His eyes are sunken and black, and if it's possible, the five-minute trip to the McDonald's drive-thru has made his cheeks collapse even further. In an attempt to soften the blow and cover up my disastrous choice of words, I add, "You should try to get a bit of shut-eye. You'll feel better."

With a weak sort of smile that almost says he knows I'm being a bit wide with him, he says, "I cannae sleep."

He takes his McDonald's bag into the kitchen where he resumes residence at the breakfast counter. During his lunch assignment he must've taken a detour via the newsagents because he's come back with different papers. After he's seated and comfy, he starts on the first one, licking his thumb as he flicks through the pages. This leaves me and Auntie Helen in the living room; me back on that leather pouffé, her on the only seat that hasn't been taken apart.

I tuck into my burger, and as I sit and chew and stare up at the wee stork ornament that somehow continues to survive the bagging, I'm reminded about the weird thing auld Harry from down the stairs said earlier, a few million years ago.

Once again, though, the opportunity presents itself a second too late, and Auntie Helen's already taken the wheel.

"Yer Uncle Raymond's never been much ae a talker," she says, easily loud enough for him to hear.

"Aye?" My eyebrows are halfway up my forehead and I ask this like Uncle Raymond being a quiet wee soul is the most outlandish suggestion imaginable, like I've been praying for him to shut the fuck up all day.

"Strong, silent type." She looks lovingly towards the kitchen and then like she remembers something painful, she shifts her gaze to her feet. After a few seconds, she bursts out laughing, and her eyes meet mine again. "Did I ever tell ye about the day me and yer Uncle Raymond first started going out?"

I can't help but smile. "I don't think you have, no."

"Me and Raymond were in the same year at school. Same year and same classes, except for when the lassies had Domestic Science, and the laddies had Woodwork and Metalwork and stuff like that."

NO WOOD.

NO METAL.

I blink it away.

—He's no gonnae get to see the wee yin.

She goes on. "Anyway, if I'm honest, most ae the time I'm sure we didnae know each other existed, 'til this one day in English. Now, our English teacher was a right doughball, total zoomer. Ure was his name. We called him Min." She laughs at the childishness. "Anyway, auld Min Ure was deaf in one ear. I cannae mind which one." Her fingers come up and point at each of her ears in turn as she tries to work it out. "The left. It was the left. Aye, 'cause when he was standing at the blackboard writing away with his right hand, he'd have his deaf lug pointing at the class."

My smile broadens. She's smiling too.

"Okay," I say. "Go on."

"So once the kids worked this out, they started taking advantage ae it for a bit ae fun." She chortles. "And what we did was..." She chortles again. "We'd call him names. It's so immature."

"Just names?"

"Aye. Well, aye. But it was the way they'd do it, y'see. Min would be scribbling some shite on the blackboard, and one of the boys would say—just at a normal volume like we're talking right now—they'd say something like, 'Ye reek ae shite, sir.'"

I laugh. I can't help myself.

"Min wouldn't really hear it properly, but he'd still manage tae pick up 'sir' and turn round tae face the class. 'Yes?' he'd ask, and the boy that had just told him he reeked ae shite would say, 'Do you have a spare pencil, sir?' or something like that. Dead posh, ken? Kinda like how you talk, no offence."

"None taken."

"So on it would go and all the laddies would be ripping the pure pish out ae auld Min Ure without him having the first clue about it."

"What else would they say?" I ask. Even though she had another little dig at how I talk, I'm enjoying hearing Auntie

Helen swear now that it's not directed at me.

"All sorts ae childish things. 'Are you a kiddie-fiddler, sir?' and 'Yer a stupid fanny, sir,' and 'Kiss ma spotty arse, sir.' I'm sure ye get the idea. Any road, Min would never hear what came before the 'sir' bit and when he turned round tae get them tae repeat themselves, they'd ask him tae explain something again or ask for a loan ae a pencil sharpener or if they could go tae the toilet. Everyone kent about it. Everyone was in on it."

I nod and take a quiet sip of my drink.

"So it got tae the stage that all the laddies in the class had done it and even a few ae the braver lassies had joined in. All the laddies except..." She hikes a thumb towards Uncle Raymond. "...our Harpo over there. And of course, the other laddies were egging him on, but nope, he wasn't for doing it. Point blank refused. Days went by. Weeks went by. Still they try tae talk yer Uncle Raymond into doing it, and still he refuses. Eventually, after weeks ae pure torment, he caves in and agrees. He's gonnae dae it. So, English comes round, and we're all like hens in hot girdles, dead excited waiting for it. This is it. This is Raymond's big moment."

"So what did he say?" It's weird talking about Uncle Raymond as though he's not here, but it's also funny, so I go along with it.

"Well, he's sweating, and he's looking ill, and there's nae colour in his cheeks, clearly letting the nerves get the better ae him but underneath it all there's a determination about him. Halfway through the class, Min's up at the blackboard as per. Raymond takes a deep breath, shoves his chair back, stands up and shouts, 'Sir!' Min turns round and says, 'Yes?' And the whole class is looking at Raymond. The whole class kens he's fucked it up, he's got it wrong, he's said 'sir' first, not last. So he's left standing there, sweat absolutely lashing out ae him now that he's sussed he's fucked it up good and proper. Everyone's staring at him. Min's wondering what's going on. The class has never been this quiet. There's not a peep out ae a living soul in that room. Time stands still. Then Raymond takes another deep breath and shouts, 'Yer a cunt!'"

Auntie Helen and I crease up. Uncle Raymond, still sitting at the breakfast counter with his newspapers, coughs, licks his thumb and turns a page.

"So what happened?"

"Well even with one gammy lug, Min wasnae that deaf. Raymond got six ae the best in front ae the whole class. Poor laddie was greeting his eyes out after three. But after it was all done, I felt sorry for him, what with him trying his best, and I suppose I'd developed a wee thing for him anyway, so I asked him out." She slaps her hands down on to the tops of her legs. "And here we are. We've been through some amount ae shite over the years but he was my first true love back then, and he's my first true love still."

Right then—right at that moment—I remember exactly what it was like to be young, to be a bairn, to have family around me all the time, to smell Hubba-Bubba in the corridor at school, to fancy somebody for the first time, to be part of something and to remember what it was like to love my Auntie Helen.

"He got some stick from the other laddies," she says with a sigh, after we've calmed down again. "Yer father probably was one ae the worst when he caught wind of it. They were great friends as well as brothers, thick as thieves most of the time, but that didnae stop yer father retelling the story in his best man's speech. Raymond just sat and smiled and gave my hand a wee squeeze under the table.

"So, aye. Raymond may be many a thing, but a talker is not one ae them. I remember one New Year at yer auld house. I think you had started the big school and we all turned up at yer mother and father's. I remember our Raymond was singing along with some party record, and yer mother was sure he was drunk, but he wasn't and yer mother whispered to yer father that it was unusual to hear Raymond so much. And somehow Raymond heard ae this, and that was him. He stopped singing. He got our coats, and we left. Yer dad was fucking fuming at yer mother about that. They didnae talk for days. Ye remember that, Adam?"

I remember that New Year alright. That New Year was

the one where I pretended to be the perfect host and a great wee help to my mum and dad by taking folks' empties to the bin for them, but I'd secretly drink the dregs out of their tins and tumblers. And despite doing that all night, I didn't get in the least bit drunk. When the bells came round, I didn't feel any different. So maybe I was busy or doing something else or not in the room for whatever reason, because in all honesty, I can't remember a single thing about that incident. As far as I'm concerned, none of that happened.

10

The news is on the TV again while we polish off the rest of our lunch, but it's old news. The garden on Aitchison Drive is still attracting the most attention, but it seems that we've all grown bored of the earthquake already. Seems sometimes that a meteor could land on the London Road in Glasgow in the morning and by the afternoon a new Celtic signing would be pulling in the crowds and cameras.

There's not much more to be done in the flat and without the junk and the clutter, the temperature has dropped a few more degrees, and now every sound echoes off the walls like we're in a canyon in the Wild West.

It took ten years to get this place into the state it was in this morning. Six hours later and it's pretty much a shell. That's all it took to untie the threads of a life. Six hours.

"Two more cowp runs and that should dae it," Auntie Helen says.

"Two?" I look around to see what we've missed. I can't see where the other bags' worth of junk is going to come from.

Auntie Helen points to a door over my shoulder. "Yer father's bedroom," she says.

"His room? Of course." I don't recall seeing this door before, but I guess it stands to reason that he would need some place to sleep. It's observational skills like this that make me such a hot-shot journo. To make up for it, I notice the ornament that resolutely refuses to leave the mantel. "We'll have room for the wee stork, I'd imagine."

"His stork. Ken, I reckon that's the only ornament he ever bought for himself. Everything else was from yer auld house or inherited from yer grandparents or bought by yer mother. If I'm honest, I always thought it was a bit weird. What's a divorced man wanting with a stork ornament? But he seemed tae love the ugly thing."

"He loved his Egyptian stuff," I say. "The books from earlier on, the camel stencil in the lavvy, all that stuff? I think the stork's part of that."

"He loved his what?"

"Nothing." I get that feeling that I've stuck my foot in it again. "Look, I don't have to take it right away, obviously. It's just—"

"No," she says firmly. "It needs tae go."

"Aye, but it doesn't need to go right this minute. It can wait, if you'd rather." I'm overcompensating with the overcompensating. I can't help it.

"It needs tae go today, Adam. It all needs tae go today, 'cause I'll tell ye this, I came here twice a week, every week for ten year tidying up at the back ae him. I'm fucking sure I'll be buggered if I'm doing it now he's deid."

She's getting agitated and loud again, and I feel powerless to stop her so I physically have to take a step back.

"Rain, shine, snow, hailystanes, and in all weathers in between. Christmas Day, New Year's Day, birthdays, you name it. Twice a week, Wednesdays and Sundays and never...not once...did he let me go in there. He said he'd take care ae it himself and after a while, I stopped taking offence. What difference should it make tae me if he wanted tae be weird? I mean, we're family, but we're not blood. Why should I care?"

She smiles, but she doesn't laugh. I do neither. In the moments that we allow to pass and build up, she breaks down a wee bit. The lip that's been stiff or snarling all day finally twitches. It's not a lot. It's not a full-fledged tremble or wobble. But it's there.

"I'll take care of it," I say. It feels like nothing, but someone needs to say something to take the sting out of this state of affairs and Uncle Raymond doesn't look like he's about to step up.

She pauses while she stares at me like she's checking to see if I'm on the wind up with her if I'm pulling some kind of Min Ure style scam.

"Are ye sure?"

"Sure I'm sure. No one ever told me I couldn't go in there."

For a second, I think she's about to fling her arms around me. Her expression, her body language; everything points to it. When I was a kid, a big warm hug from Auntie Helen was an insight into how a tube of toothpaste feels, but looking at her now, despite the work she's put in today, her arms look flabby and weak.

I don't know if I'm relieved or disappointed—and I don't even know why I'd feel either—when whatever I thought I saw in her vanishes, and that connection I was starting to feel over the lunchtime burgers is rewired or is really just a jumbled fucking mess after all. What was fragility and desperation five seconds ago is now masked with a scowl and the top lip is concrete again. And then the alarm that was previously warning me of an incoming hug has changed its tune and now it's telling me one thing, something completely different: she doesn't trust me.

NO PLASTICS.

"Raymond," she barks. "Cowp."

11

ack in the old Fiesta, I stare out the passenger window at grey streets I'd swear had wider pavements when I was a kid. In fact, this bit of town, the bit that used to be my whole universe back when I was a bairn, feels small, encroaching, suffocating. The town's like one of Auntie Helen's big warm hugs, I decide, and the thought makes me sigh.

In my lap, I've got the stork ornament and even though I hadn't laid eyes on the thing until today, it already feels wrong for it to be anywhere else other than on the mantel. It's heavier that it appeared, sharp and pointy in places and very detailed. Despite where it's going, Auntie Helen insisted on wrapping it up in a few sheets of Uncle Raymond's newspaper so it "widnae get damaged." And if that's not mental enough, it's riding shotgun with me because I rescued it from the black bag for the exact same reason. So it sits on my lap, and I'm almost caressing it through the paper while I stare out the window. Any crazier, and I'd be whispering in its ear, assuring it that everything's going to be okay.

But this isn't the strange thing that happens next. The strange thing that happens next is Uncle Raymond taking a left when he should've take a right at the West Church crossroads, and now we're driving away from the dump.

"Uncle Raymond, where we going? I thought we were

going to the cowp."

He ignores me.

We pass through the town centre and head out towards the council estate that runs near the canal. That's when the penny drops.

"Are we going to that house on Aitchison Drive?"

"I need tae check something," Uncle Raymond says.

"You want to check out the big hole in the ground?"

He doesn't answer, and as I watch him and we go through traffic lights and junctions, I notice that his eyes never leave the road. He doesn't check his mirrors. He barely even blinks.

Eventually, when I couldn't swear that I'd even asked my last question out loud, he pulls over at the kerbside, takes off his seatbelt and turns to face me.

"I've been having dreams," he says.

"I thought you said you haven't been sleeping?" I don't ask this to accuse him of anything; it's just that I don't understand.

"I'm not."

He offers nothing more in terms of an explanation and gets out of the car, leaving me to wonder what kind of waking dreams are tormenting Uncle Raymond. The keys are left in the ignition. I could quite easily hop over into the driver's seat and be back with Caroline in half an hour. Maybe I do have some journalistic instincts in me after all because instead of doing that, I take off my seatbelt.

It's not until I get out to join him that I notice how busy Aitchison Drive is for mid-afternoon on a Wednesday—it's Wednesday. Oh, thank God—and we've managed to snare one of the few spaces on the roadside. The rest of the street is filled with cars, most of them too posh to be from around here. Near the middle of the street, just about where Uncle Raymond seems to be marching towards, there's a news-van with a massive dish perched on its roof, looking so top-heavy that a sudden gust or a perching sparrow might be enough to topple it over.

I jog to catch up with Uncle Raymond. Along the way, I

realise I've still got that stupid stork clutched in my hand.

"Dreams about what?" I ask once I catch up with him.

"Helen was lying, by the way," he says without breaking stride.

Confused, I scrunch up my face. "Is this still about your dream?"

"About that New Year and what she said yer mother was like towards me. That didnae happen. I always got on fine with yer mother. I was yer father's best man. Top table. That wasnae just his choice. She thought I was hilarious if ye can believe that. A right funny burger, she called me. Yer Auntie Helen never forgave yer mother for leaving yer da and now...well, now she needs someone else tae blame. She needs everyone to be angry."

I'm still confused only now I can't think of anything else to ask that'll clear any of this up. So I ask something else that's been doing laps of my head.

"Do you have any idea what Harry was talking about when he said my father knew that Caroline was pregnant?" I'm surprised and relieved in equal measure to finally get this question out there.

"Harry said that?"

"Aye. Well, not exactly. Not in those words." Suddenly, it doesn't seem that clear at all, and it feels like it happened so long ago that it could be a false memory. "But that's what he meant."

Uncle Raymond frowns and he looks like he might have an answer for me.

"Who's Caroline?" he asks, and before I can answer, he's walking away, down the side of Kenny McBride's cousin's house.

12

Despite the fact that I'd been seeing it on the TV all day, I still didn't know what to expect when I caught sight of the back garden. No matter what I could've dreamt up, I think it would've been a very strange day if I'd thought it was going to be anything like what presents itself to me.

The first thing I see is the folk. I'm pretty shite at judging the size of crowds—another string to my journalistic bow—but if there are under fifty people crammed into this garden, I'd be amazed.

They're mostly friends or neighbours, I suppose. Uncle Raymond's already spotted some folk he knows, and he's standing with them, arms folded, not talking to them, just looking and absorbing what's going on. Michelle Barrowman, one of my colleagues from the paper, has her notepad out and a pencil poised over a page, but nothing is being written. She sees me, shakes her head and laughs. Then she seems to remember something, catches herself and her expression drops.

"I was sorry to hear about your dad, Adam," she says to me once I've walked over to her.

"Aye," I say, still not sure how to respond properly to commiserations. Then I feel caught like I'm plugging the school, and I feel the need to explain. "We—that's my Uncle

Raymond and me—we were on our way to the dump, getting shot of some black bags from the flat, and then my uncle...well, I think he just fancied a wee look at the crack."

"It's mad, isn't it?"

I nod. "I don't think I've seen as many folk in one back garden before."

"Health and Safety would have a fit."

A couple of policemen, both young guys, mill around the edges and council workers in yellow tabards are mingling through the crowd. None of them are actually doing anything as far as I can see, no one is actually preventing anything.

As I get closer, I spy the camera crew—cameraman, reporter, sound guy—and near to them, still in their jammies, still with wild bed hair, looking far more tired now in real life than they ever did on the TV, are the mother and son. The laddie is asleep in his mother's arms. He's a big laddie. I feel sorry for the mother.

Next up, I see the crack, and again, my father's shitey TV hasn't really done it justice. On the TV, it looked like a scar across the grass. In actuality, it's like a thirty-foot long open zip, and near the middle, it stretches out to maybe ten-foot across. When I see it, it makes me sway and twist, as though I'm trying to walk towards it and away from it at the same time, vertigo scrambling my balance. Protecting this crowd of innocents from plummeting down the crack to their deaths or very serious injury is a single traffic cone.

This is when I notice the smell. The air in the garden reeks of muck. Not so much shite, as such; just muck. It's organic and earthy. It's not a million miles away from the stink in my father's ward up at the infirmary, and that's the thought that makes me shiver.

The guy, the owner of the cracked garden, appears. He's wearing a woman's dressing gown now, all fancy and looking more like a fur coat than anything else. He's with three of his mates, and they're pivot-walking a big old mahogany wardrobe across the lawn. Out of everything else that's going on, this is what makes me pause, assess what I'm seeing, and then file it away in the folder marked 'PARTICULARLY

UNUSUAL.' The guy's peering round from the back, orchestrating the proceedings, which makes sense given that it's his garden and probably his wardrobe too.

"C'mon, boys," the guy says. "Nearly there."

"Careful, Barrie," one of his pals says. "I'm not wanting tae get too fucking near, likes."

The guy, presumably Barrie, nods. "Yer alright. Yer miles away."

From my position, Barrie is seemingly mistaking miles for a distance under twenty feet. Easily done, I guess.

I look around for Uncle Raymond to get his take on all this but he's nowhere to be seen. In my heart, I reckon he's fucked off back to the flat, and if that's the case, despite him being my ride, I'm not exactly disappointed.

Finally, with this new sense of freedom, the journalist in me gets bored with this observer role and takes over at the controls.

"What's going on?" I ask an old woman who I've ended up standing beside.

She looks at me like I'm daft. "What does it look like?"

"Well, mostly I guess it looks like four grown men are about to sacrifice a wardrobe down a hole in their garden."

"Nae flies on you, then." She takes a couple of wee side steps away from me.

At this point, the wardrobe has been placed flat on its back and Barrie and his mates are at the bottom end of it, pushing it across the lawn, inching ever closer to the widest bit of the crack. When the mahogany breaches the edge, the crowd gasps and I nearly miss hearing it because I'm gasping too.

"Bunch ae fucking choobs," Barrie's wife says in disgust while she rocks the sleeping bairn in her arms. She turns away, walks back to the house and as a parting shot she shouts, "Fucking choobs!"

There's a good foot of wardrobe hanging over the edge and the buzz in the crowd crackles as it intensifies.

"Two big pushes'll dae it, Barrie," somebody cries.

"Heave!" Barrie and his mates say in unison. "Heave!"

The leading end of the wardrobe dips and the end with the men rises and the crowd gasps again and a few nervous chuckles ripple over our heads. Barrie throws himself on his edge, pushes it down and it levels itself out again.

"Right," he says. "We ready?"

A weak, muffled mixture of "Aye," and "Ready," comes back from the crowd and I spot the cops and council workers joining in. Michelle's notepad hangs limp in her hand down by her side.

"I said, are we ready?" Barrie's milking this for all he's worth.

The crowd is happy to play along. "Aye!"

The cameraman smiles as he focusses on the scene and as I wonder what it looks like through his viewfinder and how this'll look on the TV later, another shiver ripples through me.

"Three!" Barrie shouts.

NO CARDBOARD.

"Two!" The crowd pick up the count.

NO METAL.

"One!"

NO WOOD.

"Go!"

NON RECYCLEABLE WASTE ONLY.

Barrie takes his weight off the edge of the wardrobe, steps back, and gravity takes over gradually and dramatically and as though it sinking into thick, clear treacle, the leading edge of the wardrobe pitches into the hole and once it gets beyond forty-five degrees

—There's no going back now.

like a sinking ship, it drifts smoothly and silently out of sight.

Barrie and one of his mates scamper along on their hands and knees to the edge of the crack and peer down into the hole. Whatever they see pleases them immensely, and they scramble back a few feet before getting up and hugging each other with a congratulatory cheer.

At this, the crowd goes fucking daft.

13

The celebrations seem to continue for a few minutes. Loads of pats on the back for Barrie, loads of activity near the news crew. I find myself gravitating to Barrie and his mates, drawn towards this ridiculous celebrity until I edge into earshot.

"That," says one of the mates, "is fucking outrageous, likes."

Barrie laughs.

"D'ye want tae try something bigger?" another mate asks. "My old man's got one ae them ride-on lawn mowers. Ken, the petrol ones?"

Barrie shakes his head, and then he sees me, and he must think he recognises me because his eyebrows arch and he flashes a smile. For a moment, I wonder if he's spotted me sitting at the back of the public gallery at the court while yet another one of his idiot relatives gets put away for drug dealing or passing forged twenty pound notes or, as was the case a few months ago, throwing a tin of Pedigree Chum at a policeman on horseback.

"Alright, pal?" he asks me.

I clear my throat and nod a greeting. "Did I just see what I think I just saw?"

He laughs again. "I dinnae ken. What do ye think ye saw?"

This is a repeat of the old woman from earlier, but there really is only one answer to this question. I smile, hoping to make it clear I'm aware of the madness when I reply, "I saw you and your mates feed a mahogany wardrobe into a crack in the ground."

"Aye? Is that right?"

"Pretty much."

Still grinning, Barrie shakes his head. "Ye never saw us dae that, pal."

I'm confused. "Are you sure that's not what I saw?"

"Well, if ye saw us dae that, where's the wardrobe?"

"Em...in the hole?"

His eyebrows do the talking. Is that a fact, they ask. Then he holds out a hand towards the crack in his lawn, inviting me to have a look. Aloud, he says, "It's alright, ye can crawl along on yer belly or down on yer hunkers or whatever if it's making ye queasy. We've all done it. We willnae think yer a fanny."

Flashes of hysterical laughter and deathly, serious silence alternate in my head and probably across my face as I lay the wrapped-up stork on the ground and contemplate exactly what I'm about to do. But then something other than consciousness takes over. I don't know. Instinct or something. Whatever it is, I don't really feel one hundred percent in control of my limbs and control is something that really should be quite high on the list of priorities if you find yourself shuffling along to the edge of a crack that might be fifty feet deep for all you know. And yet, that's what I'm doing. I'm crouching down, keeping my centre of gravity as close to the ground as I can without sliding along the grass on my belly.

I give my eyes a few seconds to adjust to the darkness when I peer into the crack. I blink quickly and often. My focus relaxes and tightens, relaxes and tightens. I find differences in the colours in the earth that allow me to find depth within the darkness. I frown. Something's wrong. My confidence picks up, and I let my hands leave the ground and cup around the sides of my eyes to block out any lights that might be distorting what I'm seeing. It makes no difference, it doesn't help, and I have to concede that I really am seeing what I think I'm seeing or rather what I'm not seeing, and what I'm not seeing is a wardrobe. I'm not seeing bits of anything that could have been bits of a wardrobe because I'm not seeing bits of anything at all. The wardrobe is gone. It's not there. There's no sign it ever was there. I've got my eyes wide open, and the only thing I can see is nothing at all.

14

"Now in my book, that's what I would call bottomless," Barrie says. He's lying on the ground next to me. His head is propped up with a hand, and he's got that same smile he seems to have been wearing all day. "What does your book say?"

I don't have to think. "My book agrees."

"Think there'll be some lucky boy in New Zealand getting a new mahogany wardrobe today?"

"I wouldn't be surprised."

"Fucking mental, eh?"

"One hundred percent, top quality, utterly fucking mental."

He chuckles just as a cold draught rushes up and out of the hole and I get an image of a Kiwi shouting back his thanks.

"Couldnae have put it better myself..." He leaves the last word drawn out and hanging, inviting me to fill that gap with my name.

"Adam," I say.

"Well put, Adam. I'm Barrie."

And so I find myself lying on the ground, shaking hands with a man who's lying next to me dressed in his jammies and his wife's fancy dressing gown that looks like a fur coat. His hand is warm, though, and as we shake it doesn't feel as stupid and before I know it, we're both smiling and laughing.

"Ye want a shot?" he asks.

"A shot?"

"Aye, a shot. D'ye want a go throwing something in?"

I have no idea why, but there's nothing on this earth right now that I want more. This excitement, however, is short-lived.

"I don't have anything to chuck in," I say.

In the hand that was shaking mine just a second or two ago, he holds out my father's stork ornament, sitting on his palm unwrapped in the middle of a sheet of newspaper.

"What about this wee chappy? We could see if he can fly if ye like? Ye dinnae ken, he might go down and came back up with an olive branch."

"I can't."

"How?"

"It's not mine. I've...I've got to take it somewhere."

Aye, I think. I've got to take it to skip number five. Was I planning on keeping it? What do I think Caroline would make of a stork ornament in our living room? Do I think she'll go for that? Do I think she'll find a braw wee cozy place for it to sit? Maybe above the TV? Or how about in the front hall so all our visitors would have to pass it? Or maybe in the bairn's room where it can keep our first born company? No. It's going to the dump. It's not going to be saved. From the moment my father died, it was doomed. This, right here, is its destiny.

"Fuck it," I say. "Give it here."

Barrie is, as usual, smiling as he hands it over to me.

And then it feels like the most natural thing in the world to stretch my arm out and reach into the hole, palm up, my fist wrapped round it, and then to allow my hand to blossom and let sunlight coat its shiny feathers one last time, to feel its weight and its angles as it rolls out of my palm, along my fingers, where it springs from my fingertips to be snatched by black gravity, where it lazily topples and tumbles as it beats its wings and accelerates away, and looking into the dark it's almost like it's taking off, falling up rather than down, flying into the night, across oceans and deserts to palm trees and paradise, and as it's swallowed up and my eyes lose it forever,

I think of limits and tolerances and calculus and x^2 and pads and pads of working and a lifetime of questions, a lifetime of the same questions, and all this forces me to make a promise to that bird, to offer a wish, that wherever it winds up, whenever it touches down, at the end of its journey when its tired wings settle for the final time, it'll find the answers.

15

When I grab the hand that appears near my head, it's Uncle Raymond who pulls me to my feet. He's standing un-fucking-believably close to the edge, and without thinking, my arm shoots round his waist so I can lead us back to a safe distance. Around us, other folk seem to be forming a queue to chuck their own garbage down the hole. Suddenly, my legs feel full of concrete, and I realise how exhausted I am, like the last few days have finally caught up with me. I've no energy, or any real desire now, to hang around and watch others go through the same ritual.

"C'mon," Uncle Raymond says, "We need tae get out ae here."

We shuffle out of the garden, on to the street and back to the car. Uncle Raymond is a bit out breath like he's been running. It's not until we're back on the road, heading for the dump, that I finally find my tongue.

"What do you make of all that, then? Was that for real?"

Uncle Raymond hums like he's not sure.

"Bottomless." I yawn and then mutter, "I tell you something, though...I am shattered."

"Aye, well ye cannae sleep yet." He sounds pissed off at something, maybe with me, I dunno. "Yer not finished. Ye told Helen ye'd clear out yer father's room."

"This isn't about the wee stork, is it? Because we were

chucking him out anyway."

"Him?"

"Him. It. Whatever."

"Did he have a name?"

"Eh?"

"Forget it."

"Did that ornament have a name? Is that what you're asking?"

"Forget it. In fact, let's forget everything about this. If Helen asks, we were held up at the cowp." He really is angry now, but he quickly cools down and says, "I'm sorry, Adam, I just...I just didnae find what I wanted. That's all."

"What was it you wanted to find?"

We've been to the dump, got rid of the bags in skip number five and are halfway home before he says another word but by this time, I've got my eyes shut, I'm pretending to be asleep, and I can convince myself he didn't say anything.

"I dinnae ken."

16

y father's bedroom door's not for budging, and I can't understand why. After all, just a week ago, he lived here. Presumably, he slept. Presumably, he slept in there.

"D'ye want me tae fetch yer Uncle Raymond from the car?" Auntie Helen asks. She's been breathing at the back of my neck again.

I ignore the offer. I don't want Uncle Raymond. I think I've had about enough of him and his weirdness for one day. In fact, I've had about all I can take of the pair of them. It would've been easy for me to leave it to them today. I don't owe them anything. I don't have to help. Yes, it would've been a shitty thing to do but they probably already think I'm a shitty sort of person whether I'm here or not.

"Adam? Adam? Will I go and see if yer Uncle Raymond's got a screwdriver or something?"

I give the door another dunt with my shoulder, but it feels thicker and more steadfast than ever. I try the doorknob which has about five degrees of give in it, nowhere near enough to turn the obstinate mechanism.

"Or maybe the pair ae youse could barge yer way through?"

There's something in the way she says this that makes me realise that I'm grinding my teeth, that I'm flushing up, that I'm fucking furious. When Uncle Raymond told me about Auntie Helen lying, I didn't think it had bothered me that much. I knew she hated my mother, more than she's ever hated me. So the lies were expected. What bothers me is her complete misjudgment of the situation with this divide and conquer bullshit. She must think me and my mother are in cahoots about this as if we're planning on scooping up whatever fortune my father had squirrelled away—and from what I've seen today, it's likely to be nuts, right enough—or we're plotting to cut her out. More than that, though, she must also think that planting her poisonous wee seeds would be enough to switch allegiance. It might well feel like I've spent the best part of my adult life in Auntie Helen's company, but less than a hundred hours ago I couldn't have told you the first thing about her. I could've walked right by her on the street, not because I was being gallus or wide or anything, but because I had no fucking clue what she looked like these days. I try to calm down, focus on the fact that after today and maybe a couple of hours on Monday, that'll be it. I'll never have to see either of them ever again. I try to calm down. I fail. I can't help it. In her words, she's not even blood. And I'm fucking fuming.

"Y'know what?" I say, careful not to look at her. "You'll never poison me against my mother. Not anymore than I've already done myself. She might have left my father, but she left me too. And she left me with a guy who couldn't look after himself, never mind a fourteen-year-old laddie, never mind how many times a week you showed up to run a duster around the place."

I feel light-headed. I take a massive breath. I feel much worse.

BOTTOMLESS.

"And as soon as he abandoned me for his bottled amnesia, he failed me. And you, Auntie Helen, you and your husband, his own brother, you both sat back and let all that happen. You failed me too. So we'll have no more talk about how I'm supposed to react to this or what my responsibilities are, and we'll dispense with the fucking eggshells you've got me walking on. I'll get through this fucking door supposing it kills me, and I'll black bag every fucking thing I find, and then you two and me will go our separate ways, we'll get on with our lives, and in a few months, it'll be like none of this ever happened. How does that grab you?"

The clock that reminds me of a spider or a beetle, bless its wee heart, couldn't give a shit if everyone in the room feels awkward. It doesn't know the meaning of uncomfortable silence. No matter what, it ticks on regardless.

"It's about teatime," she says brightly. "I was going tae suggest we got some fish suppers from Giordano's. My treat. What would ye like?"

"I'll take a sausage supper," I say. "That'll be grand, thanks."

"Nae bother."

She's never hated me as much as I hate myself and the only consolation I can take from all this is that as soon as Auntie Helen closes the front door behind her, today proves it's not quite finished with me yet because my father's bedroom door simply drifts open like it was just waiting for her to leave.

17

The room is small, grey with the blinds closed, and is so cold that the division between it and the rest of the flat is practically visible. On the plus side, it doesn't look all that cluttered. Just a bed, bedside table, small bookcase, set of drawers and a mahogany wardrobe

NO WOOD.

that's seen better days. At first glance, it doesn't look like it'll take more than a couple of hours and I should be back home before dark.

The bookcase is full of books about Egypt. As though they mean anything to me, I check along the spines. None of the names mean a thing until I reach a yellow one, kinda out of place, towards the end of the second shelf that reads: *Calculus For Dummies*.

My skin prickles into goosebumps. *Calculus For Dummies*. Just from the crease in the spine, it's obvious that the book has been read many times but the Dummies books are fairly new, or so I think. It may not have come out in the last week or two, but it's definitely not ten years old. It might not even be five years old. I pluck the book from the shelf and flick purposelessly through it and nearly miss the slivers of notepad paper fall out and drift to the floor.

Crouching down on my hunkers, I run a hand through the fallen pages like I'm shuffling playing cards. It's his handwriting—I don't know why this surprises me—but it differs from the writing on the cube in the living room. There are no equations here, no working. Just x^2 written over and over again.

As I flop down on to my arse, it occurs to me at this point that my father didn't understand what he was doing. Maybe that's too strong. Maybe he had some idea. Either way, what's clear is that he didn't really get calculus. I suppose that's obvious. If you did understand it, you wouldn't be buying yourself a book called Calculus For Dummies.

But he didn't give up. That's the important bit. He might not have understood it, but if those slabs of notepaper scattered around the flat are testament to anything, it's that he wanted to understand. He was trying. Judging by the fact that he thought every answer was x^2, it didn't look like he succeeded.

He wanted to understand.

I'm still sitting on the floor, checking out the room from this vantage point, when I see the door's ajar on the mahogany wardrobe, and the light from the cracks in the blinds is illuminating the wardrobe's floor. As I lean towards it, it looks to be empty except for an old Clark's shoebox. At first, it feels like a terrible intrusion. Then I remember where I'm sitting and that every single second that I've spent in this flat has been an intrusion and it's a bit late in the day to suddenly develop a conscience about it.

I don't have to get up. From where I am, I can just roll over and stick a hand into the wardrobe and slide the shoebox out. At some point, the box has lost its lid, but the contents look fresh enough. There's no dust, no stour. There's no sign that any of this has been here abandoned for any length of time.

On first inspection, it looks like a load of shite. There's beer labels, whisky corks, assorted souvenirs of his favourite hobby. But underneath all that, there are maybe half-a-dozen Boots photo wallets. Do people still get prints developed at Boots? Or are these just really old after all?

I'm two photos into the first set when the room starts to

spin round my head, and I drop the lot on the floor. They don't fall far so I don't upset the order too much and so minutes later, after the room has pinned itself back down, and after I've spewed a wee bit in my mouth, I'm able to pick up the photos and start where I left off.

The first time I go through the lot, I don't even look at them properly. In fact, I'm pretty sure I'm staring at the carpet and trying to look through my peripheral vision. So I'm looking and not looking at the same time. I'm braver on the second pass, but this makes me feel sick again, and I need to take a wee break.

I blank out for a while and when I start to come back, I spot some press-clippings in the box, and I see my name written in a familiar font.

It's the thought of Auntie Helen returning with the chippy that sobers me up, and I find the determination to go through the photos properly. So on the third pass, it feels like I've taken it in and what I've seen are photographs of:

—Adam dressed in university robes outside Royal Concert Hall.

—Adam holding degree inside Royal Concert Hall.

—Adam throwing mortarboard with classmates.

—Adam wearing anorak in rain in taxi queue in town.

—back of Adam's head, whereabouts unknown.

—close-up of Adam's face, smiling.

—close-up of Adam's face, half-smiling, one-eye closed.

—Adam leaning on crush barrier at lower league football game.

—Adam standing in pie queue at football game, checking mobile phone.

—Adam with friends at window table of Italian restaurant.

—Adam and Caroline in Hawaiian dress, entering pub.

—Adam in pub with face partially obscured by pint glass.

—Adam and Caroline with suitcases on trolley at Glasgow Airport main entrance.

—Adam and Caroline queued at Check-In desk.

—Adam and Caroline further along queue. Caroline

looking directly at camera.

    —Adam with Jennifer (girlfriend at uni) in unknown pub.

    —blurred image of Adam jogging in park.

    —Adam (sweaty, flushed) and Caroline kissing in park.

    —back of Caroline as she watches Adam jog away.

    —Adam crouched down, tying shoelace.

    —Adam (sweaty, shouting) and Caroline on park bench looking away.

    —Adam entering offices of local newspaper.

    —Adam and Caroline (large bump) leaving train station, taken approx. three weeks ago.

    —Harry and Adam's father laughing, sitting on the wall outside Adam's father's flat.

And then, underneath it all, I see it. Under the photos and the booze labels and the newspaper clippings, I see it. It's metal, not ceramic. Its neck is stretching out; it's mouth open like it's swallowing a fish.

Buried in the Clark's shoebox, that itself was buried in the wardrobe, that itself was trapped on the other side of a stubborn door, there it is. The ornamental stork.

18

The ringtone is long and distant. In the movies, phones are always answered in one ring, or the caller thinks to themselves, fuck this for a game of soldiers and hangs up. In real life, there doesn't seem to be as much of a rush and so the alien ring repeats and repeats.

I check my watch again and do the quick subtraction of seven and eight hours. Either way, it's not the middle of the night across there. She should be up. She should be in.

"Hello?" She sighs when she finishes her greeting as though she's bored with the conversation before it's even begun.

"Mum. It's me."

There's a pause that might be down to satellites, but I don't kid myself. She wasn't expecting to be hearing from me today.

"Adam?"

"Your one and only."

"Adam, how are you? Jeez...oh, Adam, it's good to hear from you."

"Really?"

"Sure!" She sighs again. "God, it's just...it's just..."

The line crackles, like the connection is weak and could break at any minute, like the satellite is deciding if this conversation should be allowed to happen.

"It's Dad," I say. I can't remember when I last said Dad. "He...um...he died. In the wee hours of this morning." When there's no answer, I wait. When there's still no answer, I think we've been cut off. "Mum?"

"I'm here," she says softly. "I'm...sorry. God. What happened?"

"His heart."

Gap.

Crackle.

"His what?"

"His heart. His heart."

"His heart."

Gap.

Crackle.

The faint hint of another conversation or a radio in the background.

"So, I just thought...I just thought you should know. Am I disturbing something? Should I phone back?"

"Adam, I really am sorry," she says, firmer now. "I'm not in the least bit sorry for him, but I'm sorry for you, truly I am."

"The funeral's this coming Monday. Or at least we think it's this coming Monday. I've still to speak to the Coapy."

Gap.

Convinced now that the other noise is conversation.

"Next Monday?"

"I don't suppose you'll be wanting to come over for it...we'd probably all rather have it over there but...y'know? The Coapy are sticklers for tradition. Can you come? Will you?"

"Do you want me to come back home?"

Acht, I don't really know. I've no idea what good, if any, would come from it. Except...except.

"You're my mum. And apart from anything else, I'd be grateful to have a friendly face in my corner. There should be at least one person there that doesn't hate me. Well, Caroline'll be there, I suppose. She doesn't hate me. Not yet. It would be nice for you guys to meet each other at last."

Crackle.

—He's no gonnae get tae see the wee yin.

"Tell you what, why don't you and Carol come over here after the funeral's out of the way. Take a couple of weeks, see some sun, act like big kids at Disney, the whole shooting match."

"So you're not coming over?"

"Adam, you're putting me—"

"No, it's fine. I understand."

"You're putting me in an awkward position, not least because it's really short notice and before you say anything, I know how that sounds, and you know I don't mean it that way. It's just work's really mad at the moment with the summer season about to start—"

"I understand."

"—and I really can't afford to be out of town for too long. And I've kinda dealt with all this now. Your father died for me twelve years ago. God, I don't want to sound so heartless, I really don't, but the idea of coming back terrifies me. You know what I'm like with flying."

"I understand."

"Aw, Adam, honey, please..."

"No, seriously, I understand. I knew it was a long shot. My father didn't know a single thing about calculus. Did you know that? Not a single thing."

"Adam, the line's really bad..."

"Aye, well, it's costing me a fortune, so I'd better get going and—"

"I'll try my best, okay?" she says forcefully. "I don't want you to hate me. You have my word. I'll try my best."

"Okay, well...just try. It'd be good to see you, Mum."

Gap.

I'm crying.

I hate crying.

—Folk are fannies and they fuck things up.

I hate myself for crying.

"You, too. I love you, Adam."

BOTTOMLESS.

"Okay."

"I do."
"Okay."
"I'll call you later."
"Okay. Cheerio."
NON RECYCLEABLE WASTE ONLY.
Crackle.
"Goodbye, Adam."
Gap.
Crackle.
Click.

The Book of Revelation

THINGS TO DO IN TESCO WHEN YOU'RE DEAD

1

1.1

aymond yawns as he leans against the car and lets his cigarette slowly burn down towards the filter. He's parked about as far from the supermarket entrance as possible and from where he stands, he has a perfect view of all the empty spaces. He wonders if this distance he's created could possibly be interpreted as a good sign. Probably not.

The recent rainstorm has turned the car park into an oil slick, and with the streetlights flickering as they sway in the wind, it's like the tarmac is on fire. Behind the roof of the store, the bruised and angry sky chases away the final memories of the sun.

He feels awkward in the blue-checked shirt. The metal name-tag pinned to it that reads, 'I'm Ray—I'm New! Please be patient!' just makes him feel stupid. He examines his big hands, the thick fingers and old scars and he wonders, again, how it came to this.

He hears her before he sees her. A booming beat of some homogenous dance music where everything in the treble range is overwhelmed by the bass, and then a set of headlights swing into view. After slowly cruising round the perimeter of the car park, out of all the empty spaces, the clubland Clio parks in the bay next to Raymond's rusting

Fiesta.

The headlights and the soundtrack die and a young girl slides out; pretty despite the uniform, in her early twenties, old enough to be his daughter, young enough to be his granddaughter. She presses a button on her key fob, the indicators flash, and the Clio beeps its farewells. She takes a few steps to him, her expression empty.

"Broccoli," she says.

He eyes her cautiously. For effect, he takes a slow draw from his cigarette, drops it and crushes it under his shoe even though there's still a good couple of minutes left in it. When he exhales, he's careful to blow the smoke well above her head.

"4060," he says back in a whisper.

"Conference pears."

"3017."

"Lemons."

He cocks his head, frowns. "Small, medium or large?"

"Medium. No, wait. Large."

"4958."

With a coy smile, she applauds. "Well done, sir. You've not lost yer touch."

"Like riding a horse, Miss Rebecca."

"Hm. I'm not sure about that. I couldnae have told ye there were different codes for large lemons."

"There isnae. I was winding ye up."

Rebecca punches the top of his arm, and even though she does this very lightly, the contact still gives him a jolt, wakes him up a bit.

"Cheers, Raymond," she says while she shifts from foot to foot. "That's just what I need afore our first shift... confusion."

"Confusion," he says. He wishes he hadn't wasted the remainder of that cigarette now. The shift's due to start, and he doesn't know when he'll next get a chance. He checks his watch. It's five to ten. He yawns again.

"This isnae a bus-stop," she says. "Ye waiting on something in particular?"

"Just the ground tae swallow me up."

She tuts and shakes her head. "C'mon. We cannae be late."

They walk across the empty car park and with each step, Raymond's legs become heavier as they fill with dread. This wasn't what the guy at the Job Centre had promised. Someone with Raymond's skills would be highly-sought after, the guy had said. Turns out the Job Centre guy wasn't the best of judges on such matters. Turns out the demand wasn't quite as high as anticipated. Turns out thirty-five years in the building trade gives you the skills necessary to operate a supermarket checkout between the hours of ten in the evening and six in the morning and only on a temporary basis.

"Still as grumpy about all ae this as ye were in training?" Rebecca asks while they walk.

"Yep," he replies, faux cheery. "You still annoyingly optimistic?"

"Of course! This is gonnae be great, man. It'll be quiet; it's not exactly taxing, I'll have plenty ae time tae plan out my novel."

Raymond laughs. "Aye, yer novel. I forgot about that."

"Everybody's got a novel in them. Even you, ya miserable auld bastard."

They both laugh.

She goes on, "Actually, that'd be awesome, man. Aw, man. Raymond's Big Miserable Book ae Misery. Can ye imagine?

"Hey, at least I've got experience. At least I've lived."

"What, just 'cause I'm in ma twenties, I cannae write a book? And—er—earth to Raymond. It's a novel. It's made up. I dinnae need experience tae make shite up. It's not an exam."

"Good point. Well made."

The supermarket entrance is an oasis of light. As they approach, it's not as quiet as it had looked from the opposite end of the car park. It's not exactly busy, but there's a slight flurry of activity as shoppers—alkis, Raymond suspects—stock up on their booze before the ten o'clock cut-off. Still, the general trend seems to be people leaving, and there's good reason for that, he decides. They're leaving to go home. It's nearly bedtime. The sensible place to be going right now is home. Only freaks and weirdoes go shopping after ten o'clock.

A guy, older than Raymond, is collecting trolleys and everything about his posture suggests that he's either about to finish his shift or he's going to drop down dead. He looks up when he must sense Raymond and Rebecca approach and leans over the bar on the steering trolley. They don't share smiles or words, but Raymond has to look away because the trolley jockey's eyes might have enough of a prophecy about them to send him running back to his car.

They step through the security panels and under the gust of warm air that roars from the huge fan units at the entrance. At no point during induction training did anyone mention why supermarkets insist on blasting warm air down on their customers as they enter the store, although something about stepping through has woken Raymond up, made it all real. It's like his soul, and his fight have been blown away. He's pretty sure this isn't the fan's primary purpose.

"Well," Rebecca says. "Here we go. Good luck."

"Aye. You too."

And while she walks towards the Customer Service desk, he looks again at the fan unit then down at the floor beneath and wonders where everyone's spirit goes.

1.2

Aside from Raymond and Rebecca, there's another new start—a teenager, Raymond thinks—hanging around the Customer Service desk. Raymond doesn't recognise him but he seems to know Rebecca, and they say hiya to each other and shake hands. There's a little flirting on the guy's behalf, nothing too heavy-duty but Rebecca seems to react well to it, and then the teenage guy turns to Raymond, smiles and extends a hand.

The teenager clocks the badge. "Ray?"

"Aye." Raymond takes his hand. He notices how the teenager's hand is soft and delicate and practically swallowed up in his own. He doesn't intend to give the poor guy one of those hard-man handshakes but suspects that even the slightest pressure might end up giving that impression. "Raymond."

"How are you? I'm Barney." He has one of those neutral English accents that could belong to a BBC newsreader, and he's wearing thick-framed glasses. He smells like fruit.

"Barney." Raymond smiles. "Like the Flintstones. Barney Rubble."

The smile on Barney's face wavers and the sincerity slips out of it, but it's fake for only a second and is upgraded back to its original, beaming standard almost before anyone could notice. Raymond notices, though, and then he also spots the clipboard in Barney's left hand. The question of why a new start who sounds like a BBC newsreader and smells like fruit would need to carry around a clipboard is barely allowed to stretch out in Raymond's mind before it all makes sense.

Still smiling, Barney says, "We haven't had the pleasure, but I'll be your shift supervisor for your first few days."

"Pleased tae meet ye, Barney," Raymond says, hoping that if he does a good enough job ignoring the faux pas, it'll be like it didn't happen.

Finally, the handshake breaks and Barney pivots to face Rebecca.

"Right, then," he says, "Now, normally we'd like to spend a little more time on onboarding and orientation, but we're understaffed ever so slightly tonight, so I'm going to throw you both in at the deep end if that's okay? Rebecca, if you'd like to wait here for a minute until I get Raymond to his station, that'd be great."

"Aye, sure," she says. "Nae bother. Bring it on, man."

"Good, good. Margaret will keep you company. Won't you, Mags?"

A woman with rusty hair and excessive make-up glances from the counter at the cigarette kiosk and offers the faintest of nods before her attention falls back down.

Leaving Rebecca in Margaret's capable hands, Barney leads Raymond along the line of checkouts, almost all of which are unmanned. Outside, the very last of the day's light has gone, and the window that runs the length of the store has become a giant mirror. Only halos from the streetlights give any indication that a world remains and waits on the other side.

"So, Raymond, you've been through training then?"

"Aye. Finished last week."

"How'd it go? Okay?"

"Aye, fine. Fine." Then he becomes conscious that he's speaking in short, awkward sentences, something his wife, Helen, had warned him against, so after a beat he adds, "It was very informative."

They stop at checkout 28, two short from being the furthest from the exit.

"Righty-ho," says Barney, pulling out the stool, running a finger down his clipboard. "Ray, Ray, Ray..."

"Raymond," Raymond mutters.

"Ah. Ray. Here we go."

Barney taps in some codes into the checkout's keypad, presumably logging Raymond in.

"This far up, aye?" says Raymond.

"Sorry?"

"I'm just saying, it's quite far up. Quite quiet up this neck ae the woods. This is us, aye?"

"Yeah, we like to spread our checkout staff across the store at this time of night. Don't worry. It's a Sunday going into Monday. You'll have a quiet shift to ease you into things."

Raymond takes his seat and wants to say that he would rather be busy if it was all the same to Barney. He isn't used to sitting down and staring into space for a living. He'd rather do stuff. Surely there must be something a bit more active needing done in a store this size, and perhaps Rebecca would prefer to sit at this lonely outpost and quietly contemplate that novel of hers. He's not stupid, though. He can't piss all over Barney's plan. Barney's the boss. Big Bossman Barney. Raymond keeps his mouth shut and pulls himself and his stool closer to the checkout.

"If you need anything, there's your call button. Feel free to give me a shout."

"Aye, there's one thing, Barney. The badge." He taps the little metal rectangle pinned to his breast. "It says Ray."

"It certainly does."

"I'm not too fond ae getting called Ray. D'ye think I could get one that says Raymond?"

Barney nods but manages to look confused. "I'll look into that for you."

Barney sets off back towards the Customer Service Desk and Rebecca and the rusty-haired, surly woman and he's still in Raymond's line of vision when his footsteps fall beneath the drone of the air-conditioning units overhead, and then it's almost like he was never there.

1.3

Over the next hour, Raymond's attention is focussed on three things.

The first thing is the back of the head of his closest co-worker. He counts the unmanned checkouts between them and works out that she's at #16, roughly halfway along the row. He didn't notice her while Barney led him to his checkout and he can't remember her arriving since he's been here, but he guesses he must be wrong somewhere or another. She's brunette, and her bobbed hair is so perfectly straight, it looks as though it's been ironed. Raymond judges that the back of the head belongs to a young woman, perhaps in her late teens or early twenties, maybe a student nurse or a gymslip mum, maybe still living at home and is at that age where her body clock can adapt to any situation without missing a beat. That said, she's just as likely to be in her mid-thirties, maybe supplementing her household budget with a part-time job, perhaps forced to work nights because there's not that much work around to pick and choose and she needs the money, and that's certainly a situation he's sympathetic towards. The back of her head and the highly polished sheen on her bob don't suggest her being older than, say, fifty but it's not impossible. The head doesn't move an inch the entire time he studies it so he can't even be one hundred percent certain she's alive. If asked to describe #16, he'd only be able to narrow it down to her being a possibly alive, or recently deceased, woman between the ages of nineteen and fifty-five. He's as sure as he can be that it's a woman, but he supposes in this day and age, you never can tell. That just about sums it all up. After half an hour of staring at the back of #16's head, he can't be certain of anything, and it's this realisation that pushes him towards a distraction and the second thing.

The second thing is the plastic tube that sits on a spindle under the keypad of the checkout. He's familiar with the tube because he's been through training and in a tiny font it holds the PLU codes for all the loose items in the store. He was good at PLU codes when he was in training. PLU codes would have been his Major if they had such things and this came as a bit of a surprise and a highlight of the process for him. During his years on the building site, he didn't have much cause for memory skills or item recognition beyond remembering what a brick looked like or how to mix cement, but he turned out to be something of a legend in his training group. He knew what a kiwi was (4030), he could identify an ugli fruit (4459) and seemed to already know the difference between a banana (4011) and a plantain (4235) before anyone explained the tell-tale signs. He has no idea where his capacity to memorise 4-digit codes has been hiding all these years, but it's there. Furthermore, he discovers that if he positions a ring binder so it leans against the keypad in a way that conceals the codes and if he spins the tube like a tombola, he can test himself. He does this for fifteen minutes and gets every one right. It's only when he hits beef tomatoes (3061) for the tenth time that he becomes bored, looks up and sees the third thing.

The third thing is a forty-something blonde woman, wearing a dark tan, three-quarter length fur coat that has a cream ruff around the neck and cuffs. It's maybe a little elaborate for the season, but given that it's now approaching eleven o'clock in the evening, it's not entirely out of place and not the reason Raymond focuses on her. He watches her because he's spotted that she's worming up and down the aisles with an empty basket and because she looks a little jittery. When his mind begins to fill in her backstory, it feels far more precise than the effort he concocted for #16. He decides she's an insomniac, living nearby, probably wearing pyjamas under that coat or a tracksuit. After she disappears up aisle 7, it takes her approximately a minute to emerge from 8. The journey up 9 and down 10 takes round about the same, as does the up 11 and down 12 lap. She's not stopping to look for anything, he decides. She's just walking at a consistent pace, up and down, up and down, and as his eyes take longer and longer to complete each blink and his yawning increases to the point where he gets dizzy, he begins to understand why this might help her.

—It's eleven o'clock, though. It's not three in the morning. Is insomnia still called insomnia before midnight? Is that not normal? Is it not just as well that folk have insomnia before midnight? Does that not prevent hundreds of accidents?

His train of thought comes to an end when the fur coat lady goes up aisle 13, and five minutes later she still hasn't appeared at the bottom of 14. His focus freed, he looks down the row of checkouts and is able to rule out #16 being dead, because she's not there anymore, and he catches himself feeling a little disappointed.

During this time, he doesn't serve or speak to a soul.

1.4

It's gone midnight when Raymond finally opens his mouth to do something other than yawn. During the break, he meets up with Rebecca in the staff room. She's stirring a mug of coffee rather too frantically for Raymond's liking but he's so pleased to be this close to another heartbeat, he's prepared to let it slide and joins her at the table.

"How's it going?" he asks.

"Great, man," she says brightly. "Thanks."

"Aye?"

"Mm." She takes a sip of coffee and adds, "It's been great. It's been fine. It's been...okay."

"What've they got ye doing?"

She shrugs. "This and that. Moving things. Counting things. You?"

Raymond just shakes his head, like he can't even be bothered going into it. He's pissed off that they haven't got him doing Rebecca's job. He'd be quite happy doing that.

"Ye'll be coming back, though?" she asks.

"Eh?"

"You'll not be packing it in or nothing?"

He's not sure how to react to this odd line of enquiry but before he can give it much thought, her eyes bulge, and she quickly puts down her mug.

"Also, also—see, I kent there was a reason why I thought it'd been great—also, I had the best bit ae inspiration when I was counting bags ae frozen chips. Ken, about my novel?"

Raymond raises his eyebrows, which triggers a yawn that he quickly stifles with a fist.

"Mind I told ye that I had a problem moving Sarah out ae her perfect relationship with Rupert?"

He nods. "I still think Rupert's a stupid name."

Dismissively, she waves a hand. "Anyway...what if, right? What if Rupert's actually been lying about his job all along and Sarah finds out?"

Raymond desperately tries to remember something relevant about the story but comes up blank.

"And I ken what yer thinking," she goes on. "And yer right, she has been tae his office, so she kens where he works, but what if all that was just a ruse? What if she went at the weekend and he'd managed to forge a security pass and get it like he owns the place? Does that not open up a chance for Sarah tae have one of them epiphany things? Ken? A moment ae clarity when she realises that character is more important than material wealth."

"That's Pretty Woman."

"No, it's a kinda reverse Pretty in Pink. Kinda. Manky in Magenta. Still, it's a no bad idea, though, eh?"

He nods. "Manky in Magenta."

"Well, that's all thanks tae the frozen chips."

Raymond toys with saying something smart—like wondering if there's anything frozen chips can't do—but he's diverted momentarily by the PLU for potatoes (3414) and by the time he settles on something that's funny without ripping too much of the pish out of her, the moment's long gone. Instead, he yawns again and gets up to make himself a drink.

He's on his second cup of coffee—no milk, lots of sugar—and thinking about heading outside for a cigarette when Barney comes into the staff room.

"Ray," Barney says.

"Raymond."

"How you finding it? Everything going okay?"

"Aye. I'm hellish bored, but."

This seems to annoy Barney, to personally offend him.

"Well, Ray, I'm sure things'll liven up for you once the carnival passes through. And, of course, now it's after midnight, we can start projecting movies on to the wall for you, to keep you entertained." He glares at Raymond, just long enough for the sarcasm to bite and then he bursts into a laugh that's too high-pitched to be infectious and lightly punches the top of Raymond's arm. "Seriously, though. It'll get better. And anyway, there's no going back now."

Raymond's eyebrows pinch into a frown. It's not the

sarcasm. It's not the second playful punch his arm has received today. It's not even the fact he's got another six hours to go. It's something else, something wrong, and he can't put his finger on it.

1.5

Back at checkout 28, there's still no sign of his colleague at #16. What Raymond does notice, though, is that there's nothing in this part of the store that will attract any customers. The booze aisle has been closed for hours and next to it is an aisle reserved for seasonal goods. At the minute, they're doing a special on barbecue equipment, hardly a must-have item at this time in the morning. He decides that any customer in the store is unlikely to get this far and so will have no reason to wind up at his checkout. Rather quickly on the tail of this realisation comes the suspicion that Big Bossman Barney isn't too shit hot at this game.

Despite this, at a quarter to one, it finally happens. Raymond's first customer is a young man, maybe twenty, dressed smart but very drunk. He puts a single Brussels sprout (4550), a small onion (4663) and a Next Customer plastic separator at the far end of the conveyor belt, forcing Raymond to press the button to brings the items closer. The drunk guy doesn't smile or give any indication that what's happening is out of the ordinary.

"Would ye like a hand with yer packing?" Raymond asks. He feels stupid saying it, but it's in the rules.

"Yer alright, pal," the drunk guy says. He makes a smootchy face, then adds, "I think I'll manage."

So Raymond weighs the sprout and taps in the PLU then does the same for the onion. The total comes to fourteen pence.

"I'm gonnae go home, and then I'm gonnae make soup," the drunk guy says proudly. He struggles to get his credit card out of his wallet and then struggles to insert it into the Chip and PIN machine. He struggles to punch in his PIN and struggles to return the card to the wallet and then the wallet to his pocket once it's done. He struggles to pull his bag open and then for a final struggling encore, he really struggles to dump his items in it.

The transaction complete, the drunk guy bids Raymond a good evening and then sways and staggers to the exit. He pauses to stand under the blast of warm air and then he's gone.

1.6

At some point, checkout #16 has become manned, and the back of the head Raymond sees is a familiar one. He tries to run through his thought processes since the drunken soup guy left to see if he can account for the distraction, but the minutes have been melting into each other, his thoughts have been too inconsequential to leave any traces and he can't be one hundred percent sure that he hasn't fallen asleep at some point. He can't be one hundred percent sure that he isn't asleep at present.

He stands up. He stretches. He enjoys the biggest, longest yawn of the day so far. He loosens his face and shakes his head so his cheeks flap against the inside of his mouth, and he only stops when his eyeballs begin to feel swollen and dense. He's pretty sure he's awake now.

And if he's awake, he has control over what happens and where he goes. He could, for example, leave his station and walk to checkout #16 and introduce himself to his colleague. He supposes he could even log himself out of #28, log into #15 and spend the rest of his shift with someone to talk to.

He could do that. More than that, though, he could leave his station, walk past #16, keep walking, go under the warm air, through the exit, across the car park, get into his beat-up Fiesta, be home in five minutes and tucked up in bed in six.

Before he can dedicate any serious brain power to contemplating these options, a movement from the aisles catches his eye. He looks up the booze aisle, remembering a comment during training where he learned that just because they stop selling alcohol at ten o'clock, the shoplifters don't necessarily operate under the same restrictions. From his position, he can only see a few feet into it, but what he can see is dead; no movement, no shadow, no noise. He has a view right down the barbecue equipment aisle and this one, like the booze one, has no life he can see.

Just as his curiosity slips and he's about to turn back to his PLU tube, it happens again; a flash of movement shoots across the side of his vision, and this time, he's quick enough to look across and see something white dash across the top of the barbecue aisle.

A quick stare down the row of checkouts confirms that #16 hasn't moved and down at the freezer unit, Rebecca points an electronic stocktaker at crispy pancakes or TV dinners or whatever, unaware of his attention.

Up the aisle, somewhere between the booze and the barbecue equipment, there's more movement, and this time, it's accompanied by a giggle, high-pitched and childish. He sees more of the figure this time, and he's sure it's in a white hoodie or a shroud.

The fourth time, he sees it clearly. A child, dressed in a white, hooded cloak, flits from one side of the aisle to the next, left to right at an astonishing pace and because the kid's feet are hidden by the length of the cloak, it's as though it's floating.

—Like a ghost.

He shivers despite the ridiculousness of the idea. Of course, it's a ghost. That's the most logical explanation, after all. It's not just a kid who's managed to escape a parent and is enjoying a run around in an empty store in the middle of the night. He shakes his head, embarrassed by himself.

Another giggle, another flit across the top of the aisle. This time, though, there's something odd, and it takes him a moment to piece it together. This last movement was also from left to right, just like the previous one and this time, there really is only a single explanation: there's got to be more than one child.

He doesn't know how long he stares up the aisle, but when a yawn that had been threatening for a while, finally breaks through, he gives up. The kids are gone and when he looks down the row of checkouts, so is #16.

1.7

At ten minutes past six, he opens his front door. Although her alarm clock doesn't go off until seven, Helen's already up, in her dressing gown, sitting at the kitchen table with a mug of tea and a half-slice of toast. She looks up when she hears the door close. When she sees him, she starts to cry.

He's about to ask what the matter is, but he already knows, so he hangs up his fleece jacket, joins her in the kitchen and doesn't say a word.

"There's tea in the pot," Helen says, her voice quiet and weak.

Raymond nods solemnly and pours himself a mug. It's only when he's pouring in the milk that he realises his hand is rattling and he wonders how long it's been like that. Holding both hands in front of him, he sees a fine vibration, not too violent, but definitely there. His hands are buzzing, as though they're being held against a fridge. He shakes them loose and takes a sip of his tea. It's strong and cold, and he wonders exactly how long it's been in the pot.

"It's not looking good, Raymond," she says.

Raymond looks at his tea.

"He's not coming out ae the antiseptic."

"Anaesthetic," Raymond corrects but he's not even sure if he says it loud enough for her to hear. Either way, she doesn't react.

"The doc says that they cannae operate again and the next forty-eight hours are critical. He says we should be preparing ourselves for the worst."

Raymond nods, still looking at his tea.

"He said the family should be prepared. That's what he said. Be prepared. Acht, Raymond are ye sure ye cannae—"

"No. I cannae. I've just started. They'll give me my jotters if I ask for time off. We need the money."

"But—"

"I cannae."

She takes a deep breath and then it's like the exchange never happened. "I'm gonnae need to tell Adam, though. I dinnae ken how I'm gonnae dae it, but I'm gonnae need to tell the laddie. It's his father, after all. He needs tae ken. And then I suppose someone'll need to tell her. Someone'll need to tell Angela."

When he hears Helen sniff, he brings his head up and sees exactly what he feared would be in his wife's face. There's sorrow, fear, anger; the whole kit and caboodle. Most of all, though, there's a plea; the need to be held, to hear someone say the right thing and make everything better. He can do the former. He doesn't think anyone can do the latter.

But the former seems good enough for now, and while he hugs her in the middle of the kitchen floor and strokes the back of her head, she breaks down.

Later, when they're sitting back at the table, drinking cold tea, she asks, "How was yer first shift?"

"It was fine," Raymond says.

At around eight o'clock, Raymond goes to bed. He lies on top of the covers, closes his eyes, listens to Helen shuffle around downstairs, tenses in preparation of a phone call that never comes and watches the shades of pink on the inside of his eyelids slowly rise towards white.

2

2.1

aymond yawns while he leans against his car and lets his cigarette slowly burn down towards the filter. He's parked in the same spot; one he's already thinking of as his usual space. When Rebecca's Clio appears minutes later, her soundtrack is playing so quietly he only hears it when she opens the door. She looks weary, and when she speaks, she sounds the same, like she's lost some of her spark.

"Avocados," she says.

"4046."

"Rhubarb."

"4745."

"Apple."

"What sort?"

A shrug. "Gala."

"4135. Are ye okay, Rebecca?"

She scratches her head. "Aye, I'm just a bit sleepy, I'll be fine. I've spent the whole day thinking this was Thursday, but it's not, is it?"

"No."

"It's Monday, isn't it?"

"Aye."

"And it was Monday when we went home after the last shift, eh? And that's us back for more?"

"Aye."

"For fuck's sake, man." Her hands are stuffed into her pockets as she kicks a stone across the car park. "After that shift last night, the least it could do is have the decency tae be Thursday."

She sneaks the sort of look at him that suggests she thinks he'll be laughing or smiling, but he's not.

"So what about you," she asks. "Are you okay? 'Cause ye dinnae look okay."

"Just the same. Wishing it was Thursday." He sighs because he's not sure he wants to talk about this, but it's been building over the last twenty-four hours, festering with each hour of waking sedation he endured on top of his bed covers, and maybe his original question was inviting the return. "I dinnae ken how well I'm adapting tae this."

"How come?"

"I dinnae ken. It's just...I'm kinda beyond tired, ken? I'm so jittery. And my eyes are playing tricks on me." He leaves this fact to the end, almost hoping that it will slip through unnoticed.

"What sort ae tricks?"

He sighs again, allowing it to develop into a groan. "Ocht, I dinnae...did ye see the wife that was on number sixteen last night?"

"I'm not sure. What did she look like?"

"Dark hair, brunette, bobbed. Really, really straight. Like it was ironed."

"What about her face?"

"I never saw her face. I just saw the back of her head. That's no right, is it? To sit with yer back to someone for all them hours, it's not right. And then, she kept fucking off and coming back and fucking off and coming back and I never even seen her doing any coming or going...she'd just disappear...and reappear...like she..."

Rebecca's hands shoot up and cover her mouth. "No way, man," she says.

"What?"

"No fucking way, man."

"Rebecca, what is it?" He's agitated. It's in his voice, his face, his stance. It's in every single hair on his arms that's standing to attention. For a second, simple understanding is just as good as an explanation; just to know he's not crazy, to know someone else sees what he sees.

"Ye've only just gone and seen Mergrit The Iron Bob. According to Barney, she's been haunting the supermarket for nigh on fifty year."

Disappointment—bone-crushing disappointment—and embarrassment which he decides to conceal with aggression. "Fuck off."

"Ken, rumour has it that Mergrit The Iron Bob's actually Auld Man Withers. Ken? The guy who owns the abandoned amusement park that's built on the Indian burial ground next to the buroo office?"

"I'm being serious," Raymond says. He pings his cigarette away—another one wasted—and starts the trek across the empty car park towards the store.

"Aw, Raymond. Raymond, dinnae be like that, man. I was only joking."

She has to break into a slight jog to keep up with him, and as she does, she maintains a constant stream of apology until Raymond becomes very conscious that he's fifty-odds, she's twenty-odds, and he's the one behaving like a baby. He slows down.

"I was only joking," she says again, a little out of breath. "I'm sorry."

"It disnae matter."

"I'm still sorry. I wasn't paying attention last night, but I'll pay attention the night, I promise. I'll keep an eye out."

"Yer laying it on too thick, now."

"I will, though. I promise."

He lets that sink in and judges her sincerity. "Yer a guid lassie."

And then he just wants to pretend that he hadn't opened that particular door in the first place, so he thinks of the surest way to quickly and permanently change the subject.

"Tell me," he says. "How's yer Shallow Magenta idea coming along?"

Her eyes widen, and she grabs his arm. "Well," she says, and the reset button's been pressed, and everything goes back to normal.

2.2

How the world presents itself to Raymond tonight:

Despite the promises of variety, the staff scheduling problems from yesterday have been carried forward into today, and as Monday ekes its way into Tuesday, Raymond finds himself sitting at Checkout 28, staring at the space that is usually home to the back of #16's head.

If he was more alert, he decides, in all likelihood, her absence wouldn't bother him. If anything, it should take the pressure off. So what if she was happy to sit with her back to him all night and to come and go without so much as a nod of her perfectly bobbed head? He wasn't going out of his way to break the ice with her so he couldn't expect her to make any special effort. But the fact she isn't there should mean that these points aren't even triggered in his mind. They are triggered, though. He is bothered.

But he isn't alert. He isn't thinking too rationally beyond the knowledge that each passing second takes him further away from the last time he slept. He slept on Friday, he's pretty sure of that. Saturday night was spent in the hospital while surgeons cut his brother open, moved things around and stitched him back together again. During the day on Sunday, when he should've been resting as much as possible, he was driving to and from the hospital and then he was here, in this very seat. Monday, he is here again. How long is that? Maybe 60 hours without proper sleep? He distinguishes between proper sleep, because he knows he must've napped and he can't remember a thing about driving home after his first shift, so he accepts that he probably has been sleeping, but no more than a few minutes here and there; nothing that really helps and if anything, has probably made him feel worse.

He's spooked. He happily admits it. He's spooked out, and everything in his current environment is making it worse. The hum of the air conditioning units and the fridges, sounds that are barely audible during the day, are deafening in the middle of the night once he picks up their frequency and as soon as he's tuned in, it takes a gigantic effort to distract himself long enough to tune back out. In the meantime, the drone burrows into his brain, and he convinces himself it's getting louder until he has to put a hand to the side of his head before he can be sure his ears aren't bleeding.

To make this worse, his eyes are picking up more activity just at the limits of his peripheral vision, and immediately he fears the return the white-shrouded children. Each time, though, it turns out to be old, empty cardboard placeholders thrown out from the shelves by those restocking them with new, filled ones. Last night, he noticed the carefree way they were discarded and tonight he sees the effect as the pieces of cardboard skite across the floor like curling stones.

The few customers who follow some primal instinct and end up in the store at this time are usually drunk, and once in, they steer themselves like zombies round this giant obstacle course. They bump into each other. They knock things over. Sometimes they get so lost that they give up, stand in the middle of the floor and cry. Sometimes they fight. Sometimes—like right now, for example—they gather provisions and plastic party cutlery, make themselves comfortable and prepare a quick snack to fend off the munchies. Tonight's guy has been in the wars and his nose— or someone else's—has bled down his white shirt. He sits cross-legged near the express checkouts, using his hands to smear margarine or mayonnaise over a torn-open baguette, dozens of packets of cold meat and crisps lying at his side. The store's security guard, Polish and built like a block of flats, must be struggling with his own demons and takes a moment to notice what's going on. Once he does, though, he's quick to drag the rogue sandwich maker to the exit and discard him like garbage into the night.

Oddly, though, Raymond's served more people in a couple of hours tonight than he did during the whole of his last shift. That isn't an awfully big number, but he's keen to adopt a half-full approach to the situation whenever he gets the chance. When he serves these people—again, mostly drunk, stoned, glued, wired, whatever—he disguises his fear and compensates for how lousy he's feeling by being astonishingly bright and cheerful towards them. He smiles when he greets them and always asks how they're doing, positively sings when he asks if they want a hand with their packing and although most of them can't or refuse to talk back, he engages in conversation about the recent storms, about the generous price of the dry-roasted peanuts that sit on the conveyor belt, about how delicious their day-old, yellow-labeled chocolate muffin looks, about how he can't wait for the summer and the lighter nights. He asks them if that's everything they need tonight, and helps them negotiate their cards into the Chip and PIN machine or sort out the shrapnel dumped from their back pockets without complaint. And once all the business has been taken care of and pleasantries are drawing to a close, he invites each of them to be sure to enjoy the rest of their morning. He's conscious of doing this because even though he finds the sound of his own voice unsettling, he doesn't want them to leave. He doesn't want to be left alone in case #16 comes back.

This is how the world presents itself to Raymond tonight.

2.3

On a break and in the staff room, the first thing Rebecca says to him is, "Do ye think this is a McJob?"

"Who?"

"It's not a who, it's a what."

"I've never heard of Mick Job. Dinnae think I'd talk tae him even if I had."

With a tut and then in an accent that reminds Raymond of BBC Barney Flintstone, she says, "A McJob. As in, a job at McDonald's. Man, where've ye been?"

"Rebecca, if I'm honest with ye, most ae what ye say disnae even register as English tae me."

She scowls and pretends to huff which offers enough of a silence for Raymond to pick out a rattle within the usual hum of the air conditioning units above their heads.

"A McJob, then?" he says, kickstarting her again.

"My da told me he thought I should get a proper job. I told him I'm gonnae be a writer and that is a proper job...it's not like Victorian times, I'm not fucking Mary Shelley, man, ken?"

"Mm-hm."

"So he starts going on about having a back-up plan just in case the writing thing falls through, and I could tell he was doing they stupid air quotes when he said, 'just in case,' and I told him I've already got a back-up plan. This. This is my back-up plan."

Raymond notes another difference between the two of them. This is Rebecca's back-up. As cheery as the thought is, for Raymond, he hopes that this will be the last job before he retires or dies. He doesn't want to think about which is more likely.

She goes on, "And that's when he says that this is just a McJob and five years from now, I'll not be wanting tae be still here, still moving shite from one place tae the next. I'll be wishing I had a job with prospects."

"He's got a point."

"How?" She's appalled.

He rubs his eyes. "Well, ye want to make something of yerself, don't ye?"

"Well, obviously, aye."

Raymond raises his eyebrows and cocks his head, trying a does-none-of-this-click-at-all sort of face.

"What about you, then? What was your back-up plan?"

"I didnae need a back-up plan and I certainly dinnae need one now. Folk didnae have back-up plans in my day. We had jobs. You lost yer job on Friday, you found yerself another one on Monday. We all had jobs. Some ae us were lucky enough to have careers."

"So which did you have?"

He takes a breath to answer but quickly realises he has no idea. It was both. It was neither. This doesn't do his argument much good but then he can't think of another single word to describe thirty-five years of his life because no matter which word he uses, it's in the past, he's still here, sitting up at one o'clock in the morning taking a break from doing absolutely nothing, chatting with a wee lassie who under normal circumstances wouldn't even notice he existed and at the end of a very long day, nothing much can escape the fact that Rebecca's dad is right.

Raymond clears his throat and tries to work some saliva into his mouth. He's been talking more than usual and his tongue feels like a piece of rubber flapping against a wall.

"Here's what I had. I had a pal who became a best pal who also happened tae be my brother and that guy knew someone who knew someone who owed someone a favour sort ae thing. Ye get the picture. Surprising as it may seem, Rebecca, I was no brain box at school and some ae the time it felt like I got kicked out ae more classes than I managed tae sit through. But thanks to my pal, even a useless wee toerag like me got a job that I was able tae hold on tae for thirty-five year. 'Course, that was before some cunt took half-an-hour tae decide I was too auld tae dae it anymore."

"Can he not help ye now?"

"Who? The cunt?"

"No," she says with a laugh, "I think the cunt's done quite enough. I meant yer brother. Can he not help? Ken, put yer skills tae better use?"

Raymond shakes his head and rubs his hands over the table top. "He's got his own problems at the minute."

There's a silence that Raymond hopes will hold because he doesn't know how much more he can say about this situation. He's a man's man underneath it all and crying in front of wee lassies, well, that's not really in his genetic make-up. That said, there's no telling what his exhaustion is likely to do to fuck him up even more. Sixty-odds hours without sleep and the wrong set of circumstances and he reckons it wouldn't take much to have him bawling like a baby. Despite his wishes, the silence can't hold for long. The buzz from the air conditioning units becomes overwhelming and unbearable after a very short while so if she doesn't say something soon, he's going to need to and there's no telling where that might end up.

There's a clap like a gunshot and then a voice.

"Right, folks. We're here, we're awake, we might as well do some work. There's no going back now, so get to work, if you please."

It's BBC Barney, bang on time and once again there's something about the way he says this that makes Raymond feel uneasy, like someone's dropped an ice cube down his back and then scratched a blackboard.

With a sigh and a shiver, Raymond pushes back his seat and gets up. Despite his longing for silence, he'd rather not go back to #28—and specifically the prospect of staring at #16—with his mind on such a downer, so he offers Rebecca a smile and is about to ask her the first meaningless question or make the first pointless observation that pops into his head when she goes and breaks the silence after all.

"Ye'll come back," she says.

"Eh?"

"Tomorrow. D'ye promise ye'll come back tomorrow?"

"Are ye on commission or something? We've been

through this."

"Whatever. Do ye?"

"Aye, of course. I'll not get my buroo money if I pack it in. Dinnae worry about me. I'm not going anywhere."

She looks deep into him until slowly a smile creeps over her lips and into her eyes.

"Good," she says. She pushes back her chair and gets to her feet. "Now, be a nice chap and ask me something about my novel."

A random novel-related question leaps from Raymond's lips, forgotten as quickly as it's asked, and together they pass by Barney and out of the staff room. As they walk and as Rebecca says something about Rupert's story arc and development of his voice and how Rupert might be a stupid name after all, he wonders why she reacted the way she did earlier on in the car park. The more he thinks about it, the less likely he reckons she would be to mock him under regular circumstances. She likes a laugh as much as the next person, but she's not much of a mocker. Not to him, anyway. If the car park conversation had been news to her, totally out of the blue, surely she'd be more likely to be shocked or surprised. He begins to wonder what she sees.

2.4

The yawn is so deep and so long and so warm that when Raymond opens his teary eyes towards the end of it, he's amazed that his plastic PLU tube isn't spinning itself into a blur and papers from the other side of the store aren't shooting towards his face and he doesn't have a mouthful of #16's hair. Outside, the wind chooses this moment to send a lashing crest of rain along the length of the window.

He bolts up in his chair.

#16 sits as though she hasn't moved since last night and

doesn't flinch from the sudden violence outside. She sits perfectly still and keeps her face front.

His heart tries to punch its way through his ribcage, and his eyes suck in even more light as the drone from the air conditioning boxes slips away.

—Red grapes, he thinks.

"4273," he whispers.

—Sweet potato.

"4827."

—Where did she come from?

"I dinnae ken."

—Garlic bulb.

"4611."

—Is she a wee ghosty?

"That's stupid."

—That's not an answer.

"Too bad."

—Is she a ghost?

"I dinnae ken."

—Bagels.

"9862."

—Do ye ken yer talking tae yerself?

"Do ye ken that you are too?"

—Fennel.

"4515."

—What ye gonnae do?

"I dinnae ken."

—Aside from fucking PLU numbers, ye dinnae ken very much, dae ye?

There's a giggle from the barbecue aisle. It's the same giggle as the one from yesterday. He doesn't look. At this point, he's not even sure he can move his eyes from the back of #16's head. To prove a point, he forces his eyes to look outside, through the huge, drenched window.

—Ye heard that, though, eh?

"Aye."

—A wee lassie giggling.

"It's not a lassie, is it? It could be a laddie, no?"

The rain whips across the window again, harder this time, causing the glass to ripple.

—I think we both ken it's a wee lassie.

"There's two of them, but. At least two of them."

—Yer suddenly awfy sure. Ye sticking tae that?

"Aye."

—Not just one? Ye sure?

"Maybe."

Another giggle. Another thousand gallons of rain. This time, he's sure he sees the reflection of a white flash in the window.

—Pink Lady apples.

He doesn't answer.

—Pink Lady apples.

"No," he whispers.

—Ye gonnae check it out, then?

"No."

—Well, ye need tae dae something.

And he's right. He has to do something. He feels a pulse in his arm, like an injection of pain, and it spreads through his body, forces him to his feet.

Further down the store, the Polish security guard has his head resting against his monitors as though he's been shot in the back.

Rebecca is walking towards Customer Service with cardboard place fillers stuffed under both arms.

Barney is standing at the express checkouts, staring up at him, twirling a set of keys on a coiled blue wire. They extend out, contract and then wrap round his hand, change direction and repeat. He looks like he's hypnotising himself.

The electricity builds in Raymond's body. He needs to do something, soon. He steps out from his station. Barney doesn't react. The curl of blue goes in and out, in and out. Then he realises he's poised like he's about to run across a motorway and that spurs him on, and he darts away from his checkout and into the aisle, praying he really is invisible.

2.5

The barbecue aisle is full of yellows and greens and reds. Disposable barbecues, charcoal bags, spatulas, and garden furniture fill the shelves, interspersed at an orderly randomness with cardboard cut-outs of laughing suns. Inexplicably, the suns are wearing sunglasses, which has never struck Raymond as being odd until now. All of this feels a million miles from the black weather outside—weather, he notices, he can no longer hear. Summer feels so far away.

With his skin bristling and electric, Raymond creeps further along the aisle. He glances behind him but the sight of his empty checkout in the brightness of the open floor, framed by a curtain of night, freaks him out so much he snaps to face front. The world continues to spin for seconds after his head has stopped and this is when the white shroud flashes across the top of the aisle. Then comes the giggle, only this time it's followed by a whisper.

Rooted to the spot, Raymond becomes acutely conscious of his age as his hammering heart does its best to add reminders of his lifestyle; fags, booze, more than his fair share of fry-ups. This doesn't feel like it could be his end, but would it ever? Does he expect to get a warning stronger than this? No, he should just do what he needs to do to get through the shift then leave and never come back.

—Ye cannae. Ye promised Rebecca.

"But I cannae dae this again."

—Yer talking tae yerself again. Pink Lady apples.

"Shut it."

A giggle and this time when the white shroud streaks across the top of the aisle, it moves so fast it's like it's made of light and it leaves a blue tube burned across his vision that bleeds to red before it eventually evaporates.

—There's no going back now.

Raymond remembers the image of the abandoned checkout and has to agree. He can't go back. He can't even turn back. His legs find the power to lift his feet, and he creeps on, more cautious than ever. He scans the shelves on both sides of the aisle and for all the barbecue equipment on display, there's not a single item that could be deemed as a weapon but even being unarmed isn't enough to force him back. Even though his heart now crushes the back of his throat, he has to go on.

Up into the second half of the aisle now and the barbecue items are replaced by books. At first, he thinks they're all cookbooks to go along with the theme—and some of them are—but there doesn't seem to be a solid reason for the titles on display. There's fiction, celebrity biographies of people he's never heard of, studies of Egyptian Pharaohs, dictionaries, travelogues of Southern Oregon, all jumbled in with each other. He sees one entitled Calculus For Dummies and takes the time to wonder who on earth would go to a supermarket to buy a book about mannequins.

At the top of the aisle, the world opens out, as if he's stepping from jungle to plain, and the wide expanse is suddenly overwhelming, and his eyes try to roll back in his head, and he feels his legs waver and he fights to hold on, to make sure the world doesn't drain in front his eyes. He snaps his head from side to side, his arms out for balance and just as he begins to feel more grounded, that's when he sees it.

It's not a white, hooded shroud. It isn't any number of children. The plain is empty except for one shopping trolley in the middle distance, and a statue in a fur coat behind it in the far distance and the trolley spins lazily as it glides towards him, no one in control, and it's full of something, groceries, turnips (4095) perhaps, or white cabbages (3050) and when it gets closer, he sees what it is and sees the damp, twisting red pattern that's left on the floor by its wheels and the anchor he felt threatens to break loose because in the trolley are hundreds and hundreds of identical baby doll heads, wearing hundreds of faint smiles and hundreds of pairs of glassy eyes that remain trained on him even as the trolley spins past him.

There's a giggle.

A whisper, right at his ear.

Then flashes; one, two, a thousand all blur across his vision, burning his retina, melting his eyeballs and now he hears his own cries, and it's enough to send him sprinting blindly back down the aisle, past the books and barbecue equipment. White chills to blue and blue burns to red. And still he staggers on, bouncing off the walls of the aisle until there is no wall and he stumbles over as the red fades away, leaving him sitting at checkout #28, kicking out with his legs, pushing himself back in his chair so he collides into the vacant #29, and there's a guy, frozen in the midst of unloading his basket onto the conveyor, staring at Raymond as though he's watching a ghost take a fit.

#16 is gone. Raymond knew that would be the case before he looked.

"Fucking hell, are you okay, mate?" the guy asks.

"Fine," says Raymond. "Just..." but he can't finish, and all he hears over the drone of the air conditioning units and the rumble of the conveyor belt and the howl of the storm outside and the scream of blood as it churns round his brain is the breath of the whisper that still caresses his ear.

"You turn to dust," it had said.

2.6

At five past six, as he's about to leave the store with Rebecca, he sees Helen at the entrance. The sky is dark grey at her back with only the faintest hint of daylight hiding behind the cloud.

"What's Hell's Bells doing here?" he mumbles, more to himself than to Rebecca.

"Who?" Rebecca asks.

"Helen. My wife. My Hell's Bells."

They say their goodbyes, Rebecca choosing to remind him of a promise he can't remember making, and he goes to Helen. Before he can ask, she's already speaking.

"How was yer shift?" she asks. Her eyes are red and raw, the rest of her face blanched despite a dusting of make-up. She looks like she's aged terribly in the few hours since he last saw her. "Ye seem awfy jittery."

"It..." He sees a flash of the doll's heads and scrunches up his eyes to squeeze the image away, something he's had to do every five minutes for the last few hours. "Never mind," he says. "You're here. Did ye walk?"

She nods. "I thought we could grab some breakfast before I head back up tae the infirmary."

Raymond leads her through the store to the cafeteria, which is only just in the process of opening up. There's no food ready yet so they make do with a pot of tea and take a seat in the corner. Raymond carries the tray, diligently focused on the effect the vibration in his hands has on his balance. He makes it to the table in the corner with only a couple of drops giving him away. He sits and pours out two cups that come out far too weak, but he has to do something because he's scared of what Helen has to say. The inevitable, however, can only be held back for so long.

"There's still no news," she says. Her voice is distant and monotone.

Relief. "No news is good news."

"That's what I thought. The doc, though...the doc says he needs tae start making progress soon. If he's moving in the right direction, he needs tae be waking up."

Raymond notices an irony with his own situation but the ability to articulate this feeling into words is beyond him at the moment, and besides, it's hardly an appropriate time. He resorts to the simplest of remarks. "I thought he had forty-eight hours."

"The next forty-eight hours would be critical, that's what they said, although I suppose it's really twenty-four now. I think they expected something tae happen in the meantime, either one way or the other. Standing at peace is really moving backwards, the doc said."

Helen empties a sachet of sugar into her tea and starts stirring. Raymond feels the build-up of a dozen yawns and goes over to the bundle of complimentary newspapers so he can secretly work some oxygen into his bloodstream. When he returns with a copy of The Sun, Helen's still stirring.

"Did ye get a hold of Adam?" he asks.

The question has the desired effect, and she stops stirring, tapping the spoon twice against the rim of the cup.

"Aye," she breathes out in a sigh. "I got him."

"And?"

She shrugs. "He was there last night. It was weird but...acht, it was alright, I suppose. All things considered."

"What about his mother? What about Angela?"

"That's up tae him." Her voice is the strongest it's been since they sat down when she says this. "She's not my blood. She's not yours either, for that matter. It's none ae my beeswax but I dinnae ken what she can be expected to do. Even for the fucking high-flyer that she is, she's an awfy far way away. But no, the laddie was fine. Didnae look all that upset, right enough, but it's been a long time. An awfy long time. He's trying, I suppose. Maybe he's in shock. I dinnae ken."

By this time, Raymond receives a nod from the woman on the till to let him know food is ready. Helen insists she stretches her legs and she goes to fetch them a couple of bacon rolls. While he's alone, waiting at the table, Raymond can't recall having a single thought, but now she's back, he immediately has a question.

"What day are we on, love?"

She frowns as though she's not sure or is very concerned that he doesn't know. "Tuesday," she says as she sits down.

Raymond blurts out a laugh, but it's a sound that has no humour. "Not even got the fucking decency tae be a Thursday."

Helen, who can't have the faintest idea what he's talking about, nods. "It's a disgrace," she agrees.

2.7

Raymond drops Helen off at the hospital. He can't look at the building because if he looks at the building, he might see the window he spent so long staring out of just a few days ago. He can't look at Helen because he's scared he'll see something that makes him feel worse than looking at the window. Still, he knows he can't postpone this any longer. He's about to unfasten his seatbelt when her hand finds his on the buckle.

"Raymond, dinnae be daft. Ye look like death warmed up, so ye dae. Get yerself off tae bed. Get some sleep."

He doesn't wait to be told twice and round about seven o'clock, he's home, lying on top of the covers, staring at the ceiling for a while, closing his eyes when the room begins to spin, his mind ticking through PLU numbers in an attempt to keep the images from last night at bay, his heart racing, his muscles aching, his legs jerking in spasms and he can't have been lying down for any more than a minute when Helen's alarm clock goes off and a million miles away, a million years ago, he hears himself scream at the empty house.

3

3.1

Despite being home for the best part of fifteen hours and not doing anything else during that time, somehow Raymond manages to be late leaving the house, and when he arrives at the car park, Rebecca's Clio is already in its usual spot. Rebecca is perched on the bonnet, her head in her hands.

"About time," she says when he gets out his car. She doesn't look up.

The sky is cloudless and starless, and over the hills in the distance, a storm is moving in. Raymond reckons if he had arrived any later, this conversation would be happening under an umbrella or during a sprint towards the store.

"I'm still early, though. But yer right. It's the latest I've been early so far this week."

"Parsnip."

"Rebecca ..."

"Parsnip."

"Rebecca, we dinnae have tae dae this every day."

"Parsnip."

He nods in a way that would tell her he'll play along, but

she doesn't see it because she still hasn't looked up.

"4672."

She shakes her head. "Ye could be saying anything, man. I've just realised that. Ye could be saying absolutely anything. Shiitake mushroom."

"4651."

"Pink Lady apple."

And suddenly he feels as though she's grabbed him by his temples, thrust her thumbs into his eyes, her pinkies into his ears and is trying to unscrew his head. He flinches away from the words. Perhaps stunned into a reaction from his silence, Rebecca finally lifts her head out of her hands. She has black bags under her eyes, and her hair seems greasy and matted under the unflattering streetlights.

"Pink Lady," she says.

Again, he winces away. "Are ye fucking serious?"

"What?"

"Pink Lady...fucking...apples?"

"Aye. So?"

He can't explain why. He thinks he's been taunted by this before but has no idea by whom or if he imagined it or if he's imagined imagining it. He has eighty hours worth of information to process, all backed-up somewhere, log-jammed down his spinal column, bottlenecked, beginning to decay.

"Do ye not know?" she asks. "Have I finally found yer Archimedes Elbow?"

He laughs, humourlessly, scathingly. "It's Achilles Heel, ya muppet."

She moves her hand over the top of her head and in the most detached, anticlimactic way he thinks he's ever heard, she says, "Whoosh."

He's not exactly sure what she means by this, but the giggles have started and now Rebecca, still sitting on the bonnet, joins in. They laugh until it feels forced and they can't remember why they're laughing, and then they're not making any noise, so it doesn't really matter, and then they laugh some more anyway. At some point during this, Raymond becomes convinced that he's never been as tired as this in his life and this in itself is worth a minute's laughter.

"I tell ye," Rebecca says once it's died down. "This vampire malarky's gonnae be the fucking death ae me, so it is."

And this sets them off again, and by the time Raymond has had a chance to smoke half a cigarette and walk across the car park to the store, they really are late, and it's pissing it down.

3.2

Torrential rain makes sheltered people smile. Raymond has witnessed no clearer proof of this than what he sees tonight when he and Rebecca, drenched and breathless, make it into the store. Crowded round the entrance and blocking their path, stand customers who have finished their shopping and staff who have finished their shifts. There are maybe twenty people in total, all looking out with slack-jawed grins while they wait for a break in the downpour, poised to scatter like soldiers under bombardment once the chance arrives.

Raymond doesn't smile. Instead, he grimaces as he ruffles rain from his hair, then he scowls as he manoeuvres through the crowd and away from the jets of cold air that threaten to freeze his sodden clothing to his skin. His joints scream their protest at the mere thought.

"Excuse me," Raymond mutters as he sidesteps towards the automatic gates. Behind him, he hears Rebecca chuckle, and so he fabricates a grin and tries to recapture the mood from the exchange at the car, just moments ago, when he briefly lived in a drier, more contented world.

He looks back over the heads and shoulders of those standing between him and the entrance. If anything, the rain has become heavier and appears like a blanket of cellophane billowing in a breeze while it batters the ground with such force that it drowns out the air conditioning drone. He imagines tarmac breaking and crumbling away. Through the cellophane, he pictures cars gliding down streets that have turned to rivers, eventually collecting round a whirlpool that swallows them all up, one by one. And then he thinks of his Helen, his Hell's Bells, sitting at a bedside up on the fourth floor at the infirmary while the world outside sinks. He thinks of the window.

He scrunches his eyes tightly shut until the images have been wrung out. When he opens them again, he finds himself through to the other side of the human plug, and now he's next to the security desk. With Rebecca still giggling somewhere in the middle of the crowd, it appears that Raymond and the security guard are the only people in the building not transfixed by the weather. The guard's hands are clamped protectively on the side of his precious bank of monitors, his gaze distant down the line of checkouts.

Raymond's about to say something meaningless and safe to the guard when a sudden gust of warm air bullies its way into the store, so thick that he has to take a step to the side to correct his balance and even though he's maybe thirty feet from the entrance, spits of rain still kiss his face. His hand reaches up to the moisture, and that's when he notices how alien the scene is.

No one else is reacting. The customers and clocked-off staff stand as they did when he arrived; gormless, unaware, zombified. The rumble of the rain and the distant hiccup of Rebecca's giggle are the only indications that time is moving. Everything else seems frozen. Another punch of wind sends a wave crashing into the store and those nearest the entrance are drenched but still, they don't budge, and the security guard's gaze remains distant, his face expressionless. Raymond wants to wave his hand in front of the guard's face, but he's scared that this won't generate a response either.

What Raymond sees next is very odd—he realises this before he reacts—and even though everything's odd right now, it's odd because of action rather than inaction and that makes it different. He's sure something's changed about the security guard's face; something subtle to the millionth decimal point, something on the very edge of perception and when Raymond moves closer to the guy and leans toward him as though he's about to steal a kiss, he sees it. Single grains of sand or salt are dripping from the tip of the security guard's nose. It's not a stream. It's not like an egg-timer. It's a solitary grain, every few seconds and no matter how close Raymond gets—and he's already very close—he can't see where it's coming from. As if to prove its existence, a tiny cone of grains has formed on the desk below the security monitors.

Raymond wants to say something else now—something not so meaningless, less safe—but all he can manage is, "Excuse me, pal," because there's just no sane way to finish that sentence.

When the next blast of air crashes into the store, the sand or salt

—It's sand. Ye ken it's sand. Why are ye even pretending that it might be something different?

or maybe even sugar falls in a continuous stream, still; just one granule wide and the cone on the desk rises and collapses, rises and collapses, pulsing like a heart. Without warning, the stream stops, just long enough for Raymond to take a breath, and then the security guard's whole nose slides down his face and when it hits the ridge that marks the start of the upper lip, the nose or whatever it is now, stops and cracks into three or four chunks. One by one, each chunk collapses into fine grain and then like silk, simply slips from the face until there's nothing left.

Raymond shoots back, startled as if he's a kid expecting to be blamed for causing this, his body electrified and buzzing.

Still, the guard doesn't move, and his gaze still searches out that same spot in the distance along the checkout line, but now the stare looks vacant and false. Debris tumbles around the exposed nasal cavity, most of it disappearing into the inescapable black of the hole in the middle of the guard's face.

—There's nae blood. Did ye notice?

Raymond whispers, "He looks like a..."

—Like a sphinx. Is that what yer gonnae say? A sphinx?

In the breath that escapes Raymond's lips, there are no words but the air trembles as it leaves him. When the grains that had been the security guard's eyes course down his cheeks and when the rest of his face, then his head, shatters and pours down his uniform and even when Raymond falls over, slipping on the drenched floor, and when he crashes onto the base of his spine, he still can't find any words. But when a final, massive rush of wind picks up the dust and sends it in a golden ribbon into Raymond, covering him, blinding him, discarding him to night, that's when his throat burns with his answer, but it's gagged by the sand that quickly fills his mouth, and it's nowhere near loud enough to wake him up.

3.3

When Raymond begins to come round, he thinks he's alone in the staff room, and he starts to struggle against the sense that a full panic attack is lurking around the corner. As colour and depth are added, Rebecca and Barney appear, both of them frowning as they stare at him but their presence offers calm and reassurance, despite the expressions. Raymond wonders if it's always been just the three of them. There was a woman in a fur coat, wasn't there? What happened to her? And what about #16? She's not here, either.

—Isn't she?

"Ray? How are you, Ray?" It's Barney, and even in his state, Raymond picks up the insincerity in the question.

"Raymond," Raymond mutters. His throat is dry, and his voice is raspy. "Am I deid?"

"Well, if you're dead, then we're all dead."

That doesn't help.

"You had a little incident outside," Barney continues. "How are you doing?"

Raymond nods. An incident; yes, that does ring a bell. He puts a hand on Rebecca's shoulder. "Yer not a zombie."

"I should think not," she says, fake outraged. She runs her fingers through her hair and then leans away from him, scratching the place where his hand had sat.

"The Polish security guard...is he okay?"

"It's Peter's night off, isn't it?" Rebecca says.

Barney nods. "Piotr."

"Eh?"

"His name is Piotr."

"Raymond," Raymond says.

They ignore him.

"But you're right—he's not in tonight." In a half-whisper, he says to Rebecca, "I think he's coming round properly now."

Raymond rubs his face and groans. He's not sure precisely what is generating this reaction or if it's just a general complaint but the groan is long and trembling, and he feels it in his shoes.

"That was so vivid," he says.

"What was?" Rebecca asks.

"Didn't I tell ye?"

She shakes her head. "Nothing I understood. Ye just took a whitey and then keeled."

"So vivid."

"Well," says Barney, "whatever it was, you're back with us now. It's over."

These words feel sharp to Raymond's ears. He doesn't know why, but it's happened before with Barney, and if he's sure of anything right now, it's that being freaked out should be avoided at all costs. He needs to get out of this staff room, but there's something he needs to know first.

"Is there anybody working at number sixteen?" There's no real logical progression from one subject to the next that'll be apparent to the people around him, and he's not even sure what answer he'd like to hear, but it needed to be asked.

Rebecca looks to Barney. Barney looks to his clipboard.

"At this time? What makes you think there'd be someone at number sixteen at this time? Why do you ask? Ray, are you feeling okay? Would you like to go home?"

Raymond thinks about home. The house will be empty, and he's sure that the whisper of every breeze through the trees will be converted in his head to the sound of a Polish security guard named Piotr turning to sand. All things considered, he'd rather be around people or at the very least, have some on view.

He takes stock, feels steady, so gets up. Immediately, Barney's reaching out to offer support with a hand that's holding his clipboard.

"I'm fine," Raymond insists.

"What are you doing?"

"I'm going back tae work."

"Raymond, you pretty much passed out..."

"I told ye, I'm fine. Stop fussing. It's the weather. It's dead close again the night. I'm sure that's what done it."

"Well, if you're sure..."

"I'm sure. I'll maybe go get some fresh air first, but."

"Okay. I think the fresh air thing's a good idea." Quieter, Barney says, "Rebecca, can you just confirm that you heard Ray say he was sure he was okay to go back to work?"

He had no idea he craved fresh air until he heard himself say so, but now he has a desperate urgency for it. He leaves Rebecca and Barney in the staff room, strides through the empty store, past the vacant security station, over the perfectly clean, perfectly dry floor and out into the night where he savours every intake of post-storm oxygen like it's his first and even though he's on his own, he does his very best not to cry.

3.4

Outside, it feels like it should be about time for the shift to come to an end. It also feels like it should be the weekend. It should be next week. It should be Christmas. It's just about midnight, though. Maybe it's Wednesday. It's still not got the decency to be Thursday.

"Ye alright, Raymond?" Rebecca asks. She's behind him and to the right. She stays there in the shadows, close but not intrusive.

He doesn't speak, but he nods. He'd rather not open his mouth. He doesn't know what might come out.

"Ken, Raymond, we've been pally for a few weeks now, eh? We've always got along fine. We've been through training and that and yer about the only guy out ae that lot that was my kind ae people. Ken what I mean, man?"

He nods again.

"Maybe this isnae for you. Maybe it isnae for me, neither. But ken, I can go out and dae anything. It disnae matter tae me. My mind'll always be on my novel, no matter what they get me doing. I can just about get by. But maybe it isnae for you a wee bit more. And there's nae shame in that. My da, arsehole that he is, says yer a long time deid. No sense in doing something that disnae make ye happy, and he's right. But there's even less sense doing something that speeds up the process. Ken what I mean? You go home after this, Raymond, and dinnae you come back. This is a place for ghosts or for folk that cannae see them."

He doesn't nod this time. Instead, he says, "Yer a guid lassie, Rebecca."

"Thanks." There's a pause that probably feels longer than it really is, then she asks, "Pink Lady apples?"

"4128," he says, and they go back inside.

3.5

As he walks towards Checkout #28, he realises that the store feels busier than normal. It's still pretty devoid of customers, but at least some of the staff have come out of hibernation. Youngsters—mostly uni students, he guesses—are stocking shelves, littering the floor with those cardboard placeholders for Mueller Rice and Pot Noodles and own brand cola and Anchor butter and perhaps for the first time since he started working here, he feels like he might be part of something rather than excluded from it. There's a strong chance that he's discovered another symptom of prolonged sleep deprivation: hysteria.

This makes him smile, so he bows his head, all coy, to conceal it. When he's settled down, and he allows himself to look up, he sees #16. He's not in the least bit surprised. In fact, he's quite glad. Given his new feeling of acceptance and oneness with the store, this seems fitting. As he gets closer to her, he realises this is the first time he's seen anything other than the back of her head, and he's relieved to see she's just a regular woman, in her thirties, maybe her forties, her slender face framed by that perfect, ironed brunette bob. Her complexion is pale but natural, a Marilyn-style beauty spot at the side of her mouth being the only obvious blemish. Her green eyes are focused dead ahead, and no matter how hard he stares at her, she refuses to look back.

Spurred on by the faltering knowledge that the night can't get any stranger, he decides to make the first move. It'll be for the best. And if this turns out to be his final night here, at least he'll have been able to put a full stop at the end of it.

"Good evening," he says in his best, most polite voice.

She doesn't answer, and her eyes don't flicker.

"I'm...em...I'm Raymond." He taps the badge on his breast then points to his own station further up the line as if this'll help with the introductions. "I've been working up at checkout twenty-eight, up there, for the last coupla days."

Still no reaction. Determined not to be beaten or freaked, he offers his big, thick hand. While he waits for hers in return, he notices the smoothness of the skin on her arm, still pale but remarkably warm. So warm, he suddenly feels cold. Her hands are clasped in front of her, resting on the scale pad on her station. Her fingernails are unpainted, and there's a band of pale skin round the third finger of her left hand that's bordered top and bottom by a thin pink line. Round her wrist, she has a charm bracelet with a simple, single token hanging from it. It's a bird of some sort. A stork, perhaps.

"Which I guess makes us checkout neighbours or something," he hears himself say. His hand is still extended. "Pleased tae meet ye."

And his hand is still outstretched moments later when #16, her eyes pointing forward, her posture unmoved since he arrived, opens her mouth and whispers, "You turn to dust."

He leans in. "Ex...excuse me?"

—Oh, I think ye heard her just fine.

Her eyes flash to his. Her head doesn't move, just the eyes and it's as though she's staring forward one instant and looking at him the next, without her eyes occupying any of the angles in between. There's a connection that lasts for only the briefest of moments before Raymond, shocked and stung, takes a step back and looks away.

"Sorry," he says. "I shouldnae have ..."

When he blinks, he gets a negative of an image he picks up from her, and it's one of low buildings and wide-open skies and planes and a woman in a fur coat and a hole in the ground so deep that it swallows up everything that's near it.

"I'm so sorry," he says again.

He stumbles to #28 because he doesn't think he has the power to go anywhere else right now and once there, he hopes he'll be able to convince himself that none of this has really happened.

3.6

When it starts, it almost goes unnoticed.

At first, he thinks it's the vibration in his hands, but there's something not quite right because although he's felt it for a few days, he's never been able to hear it until now. This, he thinks, can't be good.

—Is that really what ye think it is? Ye think yer hearing the vibration in yer body?

It can't be, he decides. That's just stupid. It must be thunder.

—Aye, thunder. Right enough, ye thought another storm was on the cards. But it's going on a bit too long for thunder, would ye not say?

It is going on too long, and it doesn't waver. It drones like the air conditioning, but it's all around him, and he feels it's getting louder. Not nearer, strangely enough. Just louder. He pulls himself closer to checkout 28, holding on to it like he needs the security. He looks around, waiting, helpless.

A crack to his right from the window and his head spins to meet it. In line with his checkout but much higher—maybe twenty feet from the ground—there's a silver tear in the glass, and near the middle of the tear, there's a little ball, presumably marking the centre of the impact. Surely, though, the noise wouldn't have caused the window to crack.

—Why would ye even think of that? Why would ye rule out a noise cracking glass? Is there something more obvious that you're refusing to acknowledge? Do ye really ken what's going on?

The rumble continues. It grows. It becomes fatter, thicker. It starts choking the back of his throat.

Another crack, near the same spot, and then he sees black movement on the other side of the window, catching orange along its side from the streetlights. It spins like a sycamore seed as it falls and when it lands—next to a bench at the taxi pick-up spot—it bursts into a flurry like it's unwinding and then lies still. It's a bird; a starling, he thinks. And now the rumble is definitely louder, and when he concentrates and focuses beyond the window, he spots the shadow of a globe spinning around the street lights. and when he half-shuts his eyes, he sees better and identifies what it really is: a flock of starlings. They tumble and twist over the car park, moving with the cohesive fluidity of a lava lamp, rolling across a dark slate sky that itself is flowing like a river, blown by the storm.

Another crack in the window and another starling drifts to the ground, stunned or dead. This one leaves a longer crack.

The next one, he sees before it happens. He sees the bird escape the gravity of the flock, moving at tremendous speed, slingshot around the mass, transformed into a missile and sent smashing into the glass. This bird doesn't fall. It bursts on impact, a bug on a windscreen, a dark splat of feathers and guts and bone, leaving white cracks spreading out from the centre, reaching for help, imitating life.

In the store, the lights flicker once then die.

And now he starts to panic just as the rumble increases and the window starts to shudder and the streetlights outside bend and spring-like palm trees in a hurricane and the startled alarms on the few cars in the car park scream and flash and it's lighter outside now than it is inside and in a break in the clouds it looks as though the sky is aflame, a burning dragon's eye lurking in wait.

People scream down at the far end of the store near Customer Service, and when he checks on #16, she's gone.

—Did ye expect company? We die alone, ye ken. Ye turn tae dust.

Another bird smashes into the window. And another. And then there's a furious torrent like someone's opened fire and when Raymond allows himself a peek, the glass is cracked in dozens of places, splattered with birds, raining dead starlings outside.

He gets off his chair but the ground slides beneath him and the moment his feet touch the floor, he's keeled over, down flat on his front, his head pointed towards the aisles. Barbecue equipment falls from the shelves, metal clatters and rings over the chirruping car alarms. In the further distance, he can hear tins crash and scatter, plasma TVs fall from brackets, displays deconstruct. Overhead, one of the massive air conditioning boxes takes a mournful breath and then lets out a prehistoric howl as it struggles to unhinge itself. Still, more and more birds spear into the window, and the glass can't hold, he thinks. It can't hold much longer, and there's so much glass. So much glass.

He tells himself it's not real. It's just like the Polish security guard. Just like Piotr. He'll wake up, and he'll be embarrassed for a while, but at least it's not real, and he doesn't know these people so why should he give a fuck if they think he's mental. This time, he'll let them send him home.

—It's real. #16's not there. It's real. Yer going nowhere, pal. Not yet.

"Raymond!" It's Rebecca, but it's impossible to tell how far away she is over the roar and all the commotion in the store. She's not close, he decides.

"Hold on!" he shouts back. He tries to get up again but the vibration makes the ground slippery, and his feet lose purchase. He falls back, pushing himself further from the glass but closer to the crumbling aisles. Pointlessly, he shouts, "I'm coming tae help ye!"

"Raymond!"

With his palms pointed to the ground and his arms spread out, he manages to get to one knee. The rumble is deafening, and now he can't even hear the birds smash into the window behind him, but he knows it's still happening. He doesn't know how he knows, but he knows, and as if to punish him for this knowledge, the ground bucks and he pitches on to his side, his chair clattering on top of him.

And then it stops.

It doesn't subside. The noise doesn't decrease. The rumble doesn't ease. It just stops. It's all sucked away, as though a vortex somewhere has taken a bite and swallowed it all up or maybe it was the dragon behind the clouds. The streetlights are upright and still but unlit. One by one, the car alarms fall back asleep, exhausted from their outburst. Lights in the store flicker, hum and come back on. It's not nearly as bright as it had been earlier—in truth, it's little more than mood lighting—but it's something.

"It's okay, everyone." It's Barney. He emerges from one of the aisles near Customer Service, panting for air. He drops his clipboard and stoops, his hands planted on the tops of his legs. He's taken a knock to the head, and a trickle of blood runs towards his eye. His shoulders bulge as he sucks in deep lungfuls of air. Eventually, he holds out a hand. "It's alright. It's over."

It's over.

Behind Raymond, the glass has held. He has no idea how, and it bares the remains of countless birds, splattered like paintball pellets, and webs of cracks have spread and joined and cover most of the window. But it held.

A heap of bird carcasses has collected at the bottom of the window, mostly on the pavement near the taxi pick-up point. It's a mass of black feathers, twisted beaks, and worm-like guts but as he looks at it, he realises that it's actually covering something; something lighter, something that might even be white. A snake-like head emerges from the black pile, its long beak partially open as though it's got one last thing to say. But the words don't come, and the dark eyes blink, and very quickly, Raymond has to look away because there's something far too human about what he sees. When a dark curiosity forces him to look back, the white bird has gone, and the mess of dead starlings it has risen from has parted and split like an egg.

It's over.

"Raymond," It's Rebecca again, closer now and when he turns away from the window, she's there, coming towards him. "Raymond, man, yer a fucking jinx tonight."

He smiles and allows a weak laugh to cough out of him. With the help of her hand, he pulls himself to his feet. He feels his face, head, and arms for damage, but the checks come back clear. Apart from a throb on the back of his leg thanks to the collision with the chair, he's survived unscathed. If a doctor was to look over his body, they'd never know anything had happened. But it's in his face, he suspects. It must be written across his face.

"It was you trying tae rescue me," he tells her.

"Eh?"

"It disnae matter."

It's over.

"Helen," he says, suddenly alert. "I need tae get home for Hell's Bells."

Rebecca looks as though she's about to say something, maybe offer help or a ride home, but she seems to judge his condition, realise what he needs to do, and in the end, she just nods and walks with him towards Customer Service where the rest of the staff are gathering.

—She's so warm. It was her rescuing me. She's so warm.

"It's over, guys," Barney says. "Don't panic. It's going to be okay."

Raymond hears Barney say something else, something directed at him, but he addresses it with a weak wave of the arm and leaves Rebecca to deal with it.

As he crosses the car park, he does his best to keep on top of the fact that he doesn't trust the ground anymore and the oddness of how that feels is impossible to get used to. Each ginger step is taken with the expectation that it won't hold. It'll welch on the deal. But the ground and gravity keep their end of the bargain after all, and when he eases himself into the car, still expecting to hurt in more places that he does, his relief is overwhelming. His beat-up Fiesta starts first time, its headlights picking out a herd of trolleys that must've broken free from their corral.

"Let's go," he says, and as he crunches into first gear, he knows he won't come back.

It's over.

3.7

The house is peaceful and in one piece when he gets back and it's all he can do to stop himself from running to it when he steps out of the car. During his drive home, he became trapped in a traffic jam, was deafened by some hollering intruder alarms, wasn't at all surprised by the sight of a woman in a fur coat walking slowly in the middle of the street, saw packs of stray dogs running across roads and pavements. If he thought the weirdness was going to end when he left the store, he would've been wrong, but he remained numb to it. Now he's inside, the hall is so grey, it could almost be reduced to black and white, but at least it's familiar.

"I'm home," he calls out despite the hour. He can't imagine she's asleep; not after all that. He slides out of his fleece jacket and lets it drop to the floor rather than hang it on the hook. He doesn't trust the hook. "Hullo?"

There's no answer. Of course not. He's about to head up the stairs to check on her in the bedroom when he notices that the kitchen light is on.

The kitchen is tidy, organised and empty. On the little table where they used to sit and enjoy breakfast before hospitals and night-shifts stole all that away from them, there's a toast rack. In the middle slat, instead of a slice of bread, there's a sheet of paper.

—She's left ye.

It's his first thought, but when he picks up the page, there's no Dear Raymond and he quickly realises it's not about his abandonment and the actual reason is far more obvious and upsetting.

Up at hospital, she wrote. If I'm not home before you, join me when you can. There's no rush. It's over.

Raymond sits in his chair and holds the page, the vibrations in his hands amplified through its corners. He's not reading it anymore. He's staring at the words, letting the message and its consequences sink in. He's gone. It's all over. Even though they've been waiting for days and the speculation from the doctors and surgeons has never been too encouraging, now it's here, and it's finally happened, he can't help but be beaten and kicked to the ground. He can't imagine how Helen must be feeling. She wasn't blood, but she might as well have been. Adam will be hurting too, and maybe even Angela will manage to shed a tear or two across an ocean, but he can barely picture their faces. It's only Helen he can see. It's only Helen he yearns for. His Hell's Bells.

But he can't face the car again so soon, and even if he could, his body just refuses to let it happen.

—Do as yer told.

It's Helen's voice he hears this time, snapping an order at him. It makes him smile, and even though he's alone and can allow release, he doesn't cry because, like the rest of him, his ability to mourn has shut down.

Within a minute, the page lies on the table, his head lying next to it on folded arms, and as he feels sleep approach—can almost see its light in the distance—he's very aware of his breathing and that he's counting his breaths and that he's counting down towards zero.

The Book of Journey

FEAR OF FLYING

1

There's not a single hair on his body. Not a single one. On his face, he has eyebrows, eyelashes and the thinnest of goatees, but on his body there's nothing. Nada. Zilch. Against the white sheets and pillow, he's dark like an evening shadow, but he's real. He's there. He's pretending to be asleep and must be conscious of my eyes on his skin and of the covers being bunched below his knees. I'm sure he'd like nothing more than to reach down and pull them up but that, of course, would give the game away. So. There he is. He's half my age, he's not really asleep, and there's not a single hair on his body.

The envelope marked Dante still sits angled against the mirror on the dresser. I pick it up and place it on top of the TV remote on the nightstand, but it doesn't look comfortable or secure there, so in the end, I put it back where it was and clear a few things out of the way so it looks more obvious.

After that, I'm ready, and I can't postpone it any longer. I don't take a last look or waste my time constructing a mental Kodak moment to keep me warm over the next few days. I just leave.

The brown-checked Louis Vuitton Pégase stands upright in the hallway, its handle fully extended and waiting for me like a gentleman offering his arm.

"Ye asking?" I whisper the question, the accent coming back to me from nowhere but making me smile nonetheless. "I'm dancing."

i

The sound of the phone ringing entered my dream on that Wednesday morning. The specifics aren't all that important, but generally, it had something to do with earthquakes. I'd been having similar dreams over and over for the last few weeks, of being in tall buildings with glass walls during tremors, of being in those buildings when they cracked and then collapsed or toppled over. It was something that left me unsettled and fearful and keen to find a way out of Los Angeles and to live in Manhattan until either the dreams stopped or California fell into the Pacific.

I remember being annoyed that someone was phoning me during an earthquake but before I could vent my anger on the matter, I'd woken up. The angle of the sun through the closed Venetian blinds told me it was late morning, possibly early afternoon.

"Hello?" I asked with a sigh. I was sighing at a lot of things: at the thought of losing another half-day, at the headache that would no doubt become a feature of the next few hours, at the amount of work I had to do, at the empty space next to me where Dante should've been, at a million other things.

"Mum. It's me."

I can't really explain what those three words did to me on a physical level, but emotionally it felt like twelve years of anger and pain and love and joy and regret and longing all concentrated and focused to a point maybe two seconds long. It was a feeling I experienced every time I spoke with my son. It was a suggestion that if we spoke more often, maybe the feeling would go away.

"Adam."

"Your one and only."

I sat up in bed, tried and failed to encourage some saliva into my mouth, checked the time. Eleven something. Pretty much as I'd thought. Could've been worse. Usually was.

"Adam, how are you? Jeez...oh, Adam, it's good to hear from you."

"Really?"

"Sure! God, it's just...it's just..."

Just what? It's just that it's a little out of the blue. It's just that you were the last person I was expecting to hear from this morning. It's just that Mummy is very hungover right now. It's just that Mummy has a lot of work to do, and she really should be doing it. It's just that Mummy doesn't know where her boyfriend is right now. Besides, he knew what it was really 'just,' and I doubt he'd have been in any better position to explain it. We both knew. We both wished it wasn't. That was enough.

"It's Dad," Adam said. "He...um...he died. In the wee hours of this morning." There's a pause that I spend by mostly waiting to really wake up because the conversation couldn't be happening. "Mum?"

Autopilot kicked in quickly after that and did its best to put on a brave, sympathetic voice. It knew I wanted to be the kind of mother he needed me to be right then, but he'd just opened up a whole case of memories I'd spent the last twelve years doing my best to destroy. I needed to detach myself. It was the only way. Absently, I rubbed my stomach and heard the autopilot say, "I'm here. I'm...sorry. God. What happened?"

"His heart."

The autopilot wasn't familiar with the accent. "His what?"

"His heart. His heart."

"His heart." Of course.

The line crackled and fizzed.

"So, I just thought...I just thought you should know. Am I disturbing something? Should I phone back?"

The autopilot decided that Adam was already getting pissed with this apparent woolliness and so a firmer position had to be taken. I okayed the decision.

"Adam, I really am sorry. I'm not in the least bit sorry for him, but I'm sorry for you, truly I am."

"The funeral's this coming Monday. Or at least we think it's this coming Monday. I've still to speak to the Coapy."

The autopilot looked at me for guidance on Coapy. I translated it into Co-operative fairly quickly but was sure that was a supermarket. It took a little longer to remember it also doubled as a funeral director.

"Next Monday?"

"I don't suppose you'll be wanting to come over for it...we'd probably all rather have it over there but...y'know? The Coapy are sticklers for tradition. Can you come? Will you?"

"You want me to come back home?"

All of a sudden, I wanted to climb back into that earthquake dream. It couldn't be any more surreal than the way the morning was panning out. The man I left twelve years ago was dead. My son wanted me to travel thousands of miles to attend the funeral. I was still in bed. I hadn't had any coffee. I didn't know where Dante had gotten to.

"You're my mum. And apart from anything else, I'd be grateful to have a friendly face in my corner. There should be at least one person there that doesn't hate me. Well, Caroline'll be there, I suppose. She doesn't hate me. Not yet. It would be nice for you guys to meet each other at last."

I couldn't make a decision on this right now, and when decisions can't be made, there's really only one way to go: delaying tactics.

"Tell you what, why don't you and Carol come over here after the funeral's out of the way. Take a couple of weeks, see some sun, act like big kids at Disney, the whole shooting match."

"So you're not coming over?" he asks, hurt, not wanting to let it go.

"Adam, you're putting me—"

"No, it's fine. I understand."

Delaying tactics hadn't worked. That left honesty. "You're putting me in an awkward position, not least because it's really short notice and before you say anything, I know how that sounds, and you know I don't mean it that way. It's just work's really mad at the moment with the summer season about to start—"

"I understand." He didn't. Not really.

"—and I really can't afford to be out of town for too long." Here came the nub. "And I've kinda dealt with all this now. Your father died for me twelve years ago. God, I really don't want to sound heartless. I really don't, but the idea of coming back terrifies me. You know what I'm like with flying."

And that was it. As far as I was concerned, I didn't get divorced all those years ago; I got widowed. It was done. It was over. Now, all of a sudden, according to Adam, that wasn't the case. Everything I held true needed to be exhumed just so we could bury it again.

"I understand."

"Aw, Adam, honey, please..."

"No, seriously, I understand. I knew it was a long shot. My father didn't know a single thing about calculus. Did you know that? Not a single thing."

I frowned and pushed the phone closer to my ear. "Adam, the line's really bad..."

"Aye, well, it's costing me a fortune, so I'd better get going and—"

"I'll try my best, okay?" I promised. "I don't want you to hate me. You have my word. I'll try my best."

"Okay, well...just try. It'd be good to see you, Mum."

"You, too." It felt an awful way to end the conversation. I imagined him, wherever he was, phoning me, playing with the phone cord, looking to me to say something that would make him feel better. I doubt I'd lived up to his expectations. Or maybe I had. "I love you, Adam."

"Okay."

"I do." It didn't feel enough.

"Okay."

"I'll call you later." I had to offer something.

"Okay. Cheerio."

"Goodbye, Adam."

The autopilot clocked off after that. For the next day or so, I kinda fell to pieces a little bit.

2

It's not the usual driver who picks me up. This guy seems pleasant enough, smiles as he opens the car door for me and then carries my luggage from the lobby to the trunk. He's Hispanic, carrying a little extra weight around his waist and face and he introduces himself as Jorge.

"Angela Ramsay," I say, and I reach forward to shake his hand.

"LAX, this morning, Miss Ramsay?" Jorge asks, pointlessly because I can see his job sheet taped to the dashboard and my name and destination are clear near the top. His eyes meet mine via the rear-view mirror.

"Yes, please," I tell him.

The sky and the buildings are bleached out whites and greys, and there's something strangely soothing and Scottish about the colours of the city at this time of the day before the smog burns off. It makes me wish I was up this early more often to see it before the vibrancy comes out and ruins everything.

Jorge and I share a pleasant silence while the radio, tuned to the ten o'clock morning news, whispers a prediction of seventy-two and sunny and then there's a station indent that I think I may have written, which segues neatly into Kenny G's Songbird. The silence holds as we leave Duquesne Avenue and turn down Jefferson Boulevard toward Sepulveda. I've got two hours before my flight. Plenty of time. No rush.

The best thing, I decide, about Jorge is that he's not interested and as a result, he's not talkative. Actually, that might not be true. He may well be very interested. He might see me in the back seat, pretending to fuss with something on my cell phone or a piece of imaginary fluff that's attached itself to my leather jacket, and he might convince himself he recognises me just because he knows I work for the studio. My name won't mean anything to him, though. Perhaps he wants to ask if he should know me or my work from anywhere. Maybe it's killing him that he doesn't know. He might be plucking up the nerve to ask but worried about the effect of admitting his failure to recognise a potentially famous and vain person will have on his tip. But he doesn't say a word. He doesn't ask me where I'm flying to, he doesn't make any comment about wishing he was leaving the city on vacation. He doesn't comment on my fidgeting. He doesn't tell me I look like I have a lot on my mind. He doesn't ask if I'm okay and doesn't give me the opportunity to explain that aside from everything else that's going on with work and with Dante and with dead ex-husbands and with appeasing estranged sons, my main concern at the moment is that I really, really hate flying. He does a good impression of being disinterested in all of that. Jorge just drives.

Twenty minutes after picking me up and after negotiating heavy but flowing traffic on Sepulveda, Jorge drops me at Terminal 2, fetches my luggage from the trunk, gives me his card and bids me a pleasant and safe flight. I check in at the fast-track desk and dispatch the Louis Vuitton into the dark mechanical bowels of the airport.

From there, with about ninety minutes to go before the flight is due to take off, I'm directed to another fast-track line through security and into the First Class lounge where the air-conditioning makes me wish I had a thicker shirt underneath my jacket. The complimentary bar, I note, is well-stocked.

I park myself in the corner of the lounge with a copy of USA Today that I have no intention of reading and a Bloody Mary that I most certainly have every intention of drinking. Over the next thirty minutes, I see Keanu Reeves, Helen

Mirren, Slash, Jim Belushi, a guy who I think plays in the NBA and Woody Allen. I hear boarding announcements for flights to New York, Sydney, Buenos Aires, Miami, and Paris.

I'm about to pull myself together enough to get up and ask about my flight—and maybe grab another Bloody Mary for good luck on the way back—when there's an announcement over the PA, delivered in a very matter-of-fact manner, that due to circumstances out of the airline's control, the twelve o'clock flight to London Heathrow has been cancelled.

ii

There's a house in my mind, and that house has doors. Behind those doors are cages, and the cages are stored in boxes, and the boxes are buried in concrete. Held in the cages are monsters. It had taken years of hard work to construct these levels of security, to keep the monsters at bay.

Friends—new friends—recommended therapy. They said that the healthy position would be to let the monsters loose, find a new place of mutual understanding and respect with the monsters and eventually I'd discover that they weren't monsters at all and we could all live happily ever after together. This sounded expensive. My old friends would've told me to give myself a shake and stop acting like such a fucking prima donna. I felt that my high-security mental monster storage area was something of a happy medium.

Although it didn't seem quite so bad in the moments immediately after we hung up, Adam's phone call initiated something of a mass monster break-out. I had a panic attack in the shower and another one later in the kitchen when I became convinced that the first attack had left me so far behind in my work that I'd get fired before the day was out. Somehow I held it together while 20mg of Valium shepherded the monsters back into their cages and then I spent the rest of the day lying in the foetal position on top of the covers, shivering internally but not externally, clutching my stomach.

During this time, I still had troubling thoughts and plenty to worry about, but I no longer cared. For example, it didn't escape me that it had been more than twenty-four hours since I'd seen Dante and while I convinced myself that he'd somehow been able to creep back in without me hearing and had managed to see me sobbing and broken in the corner of the shower cubicle and had promptly performed a swift bunk as a result, it wasn't enough for me to start phoning round his friends; or worse, his parents. I'd deal with it later. I was making progress.

Baby isn't my personal assistant—she isn't anyone's personal assistant—but her job is to be connected and to fix problems, and she does her job exceptionally well. So that's why, after I broke a twenty-four hour fast and with the sunlight breaking through the blinds at a familiar angle, I phoned her. The last of the Valium had left my head fuzzy and hungover, so I sounded reasonably detached and in control when I explained about Adam's call from the day before. While I spoke, she didn't interrupt, and it calmed me to think of her taking notes on the other end, making plans, putting wheels in motion, sketching out the big picture. Baby would know what I should do.

"I had no idea," she said when I finished. "I mean, I knew you were divorced, we'd talked about that. But jeez, seriously. That's kinda epic bad."

I sighed. "So. What do you think?"

"What do I think? I think you pretend that call never happened and then you go speak to your therapist."

"I don't have a therapist."

"Well, sweetheart, no wonder you're fucked up. I have the numbers for, eight, nine, literally at my fingertips. I'm looking at one right now in Culver City, about a minute away from you. Or there's one in Mar Vista if that's any better? If you'd prefer something a little further away and more private, I mean."

"I'll keep them in mind," I said with no intention of doing so. "Just ignore it, though? You think that's the way to go?"

"Sure. Why not?"

"Because he's my son. He needs me." I didn't imagine her scribbling notes anymore. I imagined her putting a hand over the phone so she could continue a conversation with someone else while I spoke.

"The only thing he needs is someone to blame," Baby said. "Look. You had to leave when you did. You had no choice. And besides, you said he got out a couple of months later."

"Two years later."

"So it wasn't like you were abandoning a child."

"He was fourteen."

"Exactly. And if you'd stayed...well, sweetie, what use would you be to any of us dead?"

That was it, though. He probably thought of me as being dead anyway. Did that make a difference one way or the other? Was that a greater incentive to prove him wrong or to reluctantly concede he was right? I didn't know.

I pinched the bridge of my nose. "For the sake of argument, can we pretend for a moment that I have an ounce of motherly instinct left in me? And can we also assume Michael's going to be okay with giving me some time off. Can we do that?"

"Sure."

"Well, on that basis, is it even possible to get back to Scotland in time for Monday?"

"Angela, it's Thursday. It's LA. It's the twenty-first century. Of course, it's possible. It's possible for you to be on a flight this afternoon if that's what you really want."

Whoa. That was a bit too close too quick. My phobias hadn't changed overnight, and the ideas of flying and of going home still terrified me. "Let's...let's make sure that it's possible first and if it is, when's the latest I have to make up my mind? I mean, presuming Sunday would be too late, but Saturday would be fine or whatever. Does that make sense?"

"Yeah, I'm on it," Baby said and once again, in my head, she was scribbling notes. I smiled. She went on, "Leave it with me, I'll make some calls, and I'll get back to you. One last thing, though. Just because you can, doesn't mean you should. Keep that in mind, sweetheart."

After we hung up, I sat at the piano and hit a few keys for a while, not really thinking about work or creating anything in particular, just making a noise. Speaking to Baby had helped; I just wished she had come up with a better collection of reasons to ignore the call to go back to Scotland and to over-ride my instinct to at least try to be a good mother.

3

For some reason, Baby is obsessed with knowing why the flight to Heathrow has been cancelled. For equally mysterious reasons, the woman who works the desk at the entrance to the lounge isn't keen on filling me in.

"How the fuck should I know?" I whisper into my cell. "They've cancelled it. That's all they'll tell me."

"Cool." She's as calm as ever. "Cool. Okay, well, hold tight."

I look round the reception of the lounge, my face a picture of surprise. Where else am I meant to go? There's a cell phone buzz that I assume is coming from Baby's end of the line.

"I know a guy who works at LAX," Baby says. "He'll let me know what's going on."

"Does it matter?" I'm trying not to sound too pissed, but it's still early, and recently, I've barely been in control of my mood at the best of times.

"It'll let us know how complicated your next few hours are going to be."

That's good. That gives me some expectations I can work with.

"What's the range?" I ask.

"The range? Well, I guess the least complicated is the flight's cancelled, there's no plans to slot a replacement in later in the day, and you decide to go home. That's probably the least complicated way this could play out."

"And the most?"

"The most? Sweetheart, imagine the most complicated day in the world. This could end up way more complicated. Seriously, the sky's the limit."

I give it some careful thought as I pinch a piece of candy from the bowl on the desk. "Somewhere on the easy end of the spectrum would be best," I say, like it's a request show.

Candy.

It's not really a strong realization, so it doesn't hit me as such. It dawns on me gradually. I guess that's the best way to describe it.

Candy. I wonder how long I've thought of it as candy as opposed to sweeties. When did a mobile become a cell? Do I think of it as aluminium or aluminum? Pavement or sidewalk? Do I have an accent? I've never really thought about it. No one's mentioned it. Has this transformation been a slow process, did it happen twelve years ago or has it just started now?

A replay of the cell phone chatter brings me back, just as Baby says, "Here we go. Let's see what's happening." Pause. She clears her throat. "Oh."

"Oh?"

"Oh."

"That's a good oh, right?"

"My guy on the ground says that in the last half hour a group of Jethro Tull fans have postponed their plans until tomorrow. And Jethro Tull themselves were also on the flight. They've also postponed—"

"I quite like Jethro Tull," I mutter.

"—and it would seem that aside from Jethro Tull, associated crew and their official fan club, the residual passenger list consists of...you."

That takes a moment to sink in. "Me?"

"You."

"Just me?"

"Just you."

"You're telling me that aside from Jethro Tull and their entourage, I'm the only person in LA wanting to fly to London?"

"On this particular day, at this particular time, by this particular airline, yes. Understandably, Air New Zealand have a policy on flying single passengers thousands of miles across a continent and an ocean. They're against it."

The idea of being on a jumbo jet on my own with my poor little Louis Vuitton pin-balling around the hold is so surreal and terrifying, I actually start to sweat. Even though the few times I've flown First Class have always been fairly solitary affairs anyway, I guess on a subconscious level I've taken comfort from the fact that if the plane was to go down or smash into a mountain, at least I wouldn't be the only one to perish. I didn't realise that dying in the company of so many strangers could play such a vital role in my phobia.

"Now," Baby says. "Like we talked about, there's another flight to Heathrow at around ten this evening—"

"Ten? Ten o'clock?"

"—but, it's still early so what we could do is switch you onto a domestic flight, get you to another hub and an alternate way back to the UK."

I look behind me at the lounge. It's pleasant enough, very clean, still well-stocked with Stoli and tomato juice but there are no windows, I notice, and the idea of spending half a day sitting around while people come and go would dement me.

"At least you'd be moving," Baby says.

And that's it exactly. Keep on moving.

"So where are you sending me?"

I can tell Baby's smiling when she asks, "By any chance, you're not wearing a flower in your hair, are you?"

iii

My five-mile drive to my meeting with Michael at Oskar in Century City should have been slow and uneventful. Although

I was more than familiar with the route, I preferred the security of letting the GPS guide me along the streets and boulevards and through the jams and gridlock. That afternoon, though, it started playing up, and when I looked at the screen, the little red pointer in the middle of the screen jumped around like a flea, so quick that the map had trouble keeping up. It wasn't just pinging around my current location. It wasn't just Los Angeles. According to the screen, in the space of a few seconds, I flitted between New York, Houston, Miami and a thousand other places I didn't recognise. Hitting the screen just made it worse.

"Take the exit," the robot lady kept saying, even when the car sat stationary at traffic lights. When it told me, "Make a U-turn," I had to turn it off because I suddenly became scared of what it might go on to say.

So I arrived at Oskar in a semi-agitated state with a very confused sense of alienation, and although I had promised myself I wouldn't drink today, the first thing I did, even before I sat down, was to order a Bloody Mary. Determined to avoid sitting alone, I hadn't left the house on time, and lunchtime traffic had helped to make me a respectable fifteen minutes late. Michael had phoned ahead and left his obligatory message with the maitre d' that he'd be another half hour. No apology. No explanation. No real surprise.

During that half hour at the usual terrace table, I stirred my drink with a black straw and blanked out the world as it passed me by. My mind kept going back to the GPS and its jumpy behavior, and I wound up thinking about co-ordinates, the x, and the y, and the z. I thought about all the people whose lives had paused momentarily while they parked themselves at this very chair over the years and those who would do so in years to come. I thought about zooming out and looking down on the twenty million people who shared the city. I imagined it as a hive until it morphed into a brain with sparks of electricity shooting around, running errands that ultimately would prove futile, pretending to be busy—one of those sparks would be Dante—but the further I pulled out, the more it became apparent that the bigger entity was itself just a dot in an even bigger picture. Somehow, that took me back through a brief reprise of my monsters in cages.

Most of all, I thought about the space I occupy in the universe. I likened myself to the marker on the GPS because infinity shot out in every direction around me, which meant I was the centre of the universe. But then I saw myself jump around until I tracked back to Scotland and being married with a kid and with a family and in-laws and how although I must've been the centre of the universe back then, too, I wasn't the same person. I wondered if there could be two centres of the universe and what these versions of myself would think of each other if they met. I didn't think they'd be friends.

"Angela." The voice came from behind me, twenty minutes late or thirty-five depending on how I chose to look at it. Hands were planted on my shoulders, a kiss on my cheek.

Michael sat down opposite me and ordered lobster spaghetti for both of us and a Californian Chardonnay, handing an unopened menu back to the waiter. He looked flustered and in a hurry, exactly the same as every other time we'd met.

"You're looking well," he said while he unfastened his suit jacket.

"Thank you. I look like shite."

He smiled and frowned. "Shite? Well, that sounds very feminine. Thank you, Angela."

"It's a long story."

"What's new in your world?" he asked.

"Same old," I replied, wondering if my voice sounded as weird to other people as it did to me at that point. "Oh, my GPS has developed dementia. That's kinda fun."

Michael grabbed a breadstick from the centre of the table and started nibbling through it like a rabbit with a carrot made from cocaine. "Baby tells me your husband died."

"Ex-husband," I corrected. "Yeah."

"I'm sorry. Baby also said he was a bit of a douchebag."

I laughed. "He—um—well, yeah, he had his moments."

We looked at each other while I tried to gauge how this was going to play out. In amongst his usual frantic demeanor, his eyebrows narrowed, and his expression became quizzical, and I got the impression that great care was being taken on his part not to say the wrong thing.

"The thing is, Michael," I said, "and Baby's probably already told you, but my son wants me home for the funeral on Monday."

"Yeah, she said. It's a tough time. If I can do anything to help..."

We reached something of a road-block at that point. He offered a smile that could've been interpreted as sympathetic but struck me as being more prompting. I'm really sorry but cut to the fucking chase, it seemed to say.

"So," I said.

"So," he agreed.

I knew his mind would already be turning to how late he was going to be for his next meeting so rather than allow the silence a chance to get awkward, he placed his hands very carefully and softly by the sides of his cutlery.

"What do you need me to say? Do you need me to green light this? Is that what this is about?"

"Well, it's my son, Michael. It's complicated. He wants me to—"

"What about you? What do you want to do? Hm?" He sat back in his chair. "I love your work. I love your attitude. You know that. Do you want me to tell you that your absence for a few days would put a little extra pressure on us? Yes, it would. Not only are you one of our best composers, you're one of our most creative and dependable, which admittedly is probably why you're so busy. Under normal circumstances would I grant you a week vacation? Of course, I wouldn't. Look, I'm a compassionate guy but I can't make up your mind for you, Angela, and what I won't do is tell you that you can't go. If that's what you're waiting on, forget it. Aside from it being a really shitty thing to do, if word got out, the union would rip me to shreds. Your conscience is your own business and these are exceptional circumstances." He shrugged and then started looking around at the other people who had decided that Oskar was the place that they were going to pretend to have lunch that day.

I tried to imagine how Baby must've pitched this to him, how I must've sounded when I spoke to Baby. I knew that a brick wall somewhere wouldn't have been the end of the world, but I didn't think I'd been so obviously looking for one.

"I want to be a good mother," I said. Right then, at that moment, I couldn't allow myself to believe in anything else.

"Then go," Michael said. "You should go."

Lunch with Michael worked out like every other lunch we've ever had: brief. When the lobster arrived, he barely touched it, and he drank maybe half a glass of wine like it was lemonade. If he could've eaten while standing up and fastening his suit button, I'm sure he would've. Over the next few minutes, we talked about how the summer schedule was shaping up and about some more work that would be coming in my direction once we'd got this month out of the way. We talked about his place in Colorado Springs that had been broken into last week, and the burglars hadn't stolen anything—and he wasn't sure if that still made them burglars—but the police had found what they described as a nest made from his wife's clothes in the middle of the living room. Then we talked about an upcoming business trip to Tahiti that would conveniently back onto his summer vacation. Or rather, he talked, and I picked up the general gist whenever I tuned in. Ten minutes after he sat down, the meeting and meal officially came to an end.

"Okay, good," he said as he tapped the sides of his mouth with his napkin. "I've helped. Your mind is made up. There's no going back now."

"Excuse me?" I don't know why I said it. I'd heard him perfectly well, but the words were out before I could do anything about it.

He pulled his wallet from his inside pocket. "You sleeping okay, Angela? How many of those have you had?" He threw some money down on the table.

"I...I've only had one."

He smiled and nodded in a way that told me he was pleased with himself for not feigning surprise. "Get a cab home."

135

4

use visualisation techniques but they've never worked in the past and it's no surprise when they don't suddenly start working now.

Lying on grass, mowing the grass, mowing the grass on a sit-in lawnmower, driving down the road in a ride-on lawnmower, driving down the road in a drag car, battering down a runway in a drag car, battering down a runway in a plane, out of control, death.

Eating an apple, eating a toffee apple, eating candy-floss, eating candy-floss at the fair, on a rollercoaster at the fair, on a rollercoaster in a plane, battering down a runway in a plane, out of control, death.

Floating in the ocean, bobbing with waves, bobbing in bigger waves, flung in the air by a tsunami, caught by a plane, bobbing along a runway in a plane, battering down the runway in a plane, out of control, death.

Reading a book, reading a magazine, reading an in-flight magazine, battering down a runway in plane, out of control, death.

It's useless. So, like always, I sit, stare at the chair in front of me and do my damnedest to rip the arms off of my seat.

"Are you okay, miss?"

"Out of control. Death."

"Excuse me?"

Without moving my head, my eyes stretch to their limits as I look at the young man next to me. His features—apart from his blond hair—are a blur.

"I'm sorry," I explain. "I'm not a very good flyer."

"Me neither. That's why I usually take a plane."

"Funny."

"I know what you mean, though. For a while, I thought the only reason planes ever took off was the collective willpower of everyone on board."

"That's cute. Do you have a whole routine worked out or—"

"Did you know that there are two separate theories of aerodynamics and—"

"Hey, you know what? This really isn't helping."

At that second, the chair tips back and it's like a cushion of air pushes us up and forward, the vibrations in this metal tube reaching the point where we're surely losing wings and engines and fuselages at an alarming rate, and even though I can feel us gain height and out of the corner of my eye I see the ground quickly drop away, I can also feel the thinness of the cushion of air, I can sense its fragility like a soggy piece of paper and then, as if to prove me right, we drop and I rise out of my seat and even though we're talking millimetres and milliseconds, there's still a moment, no matter how brief, where I am officially floating, and the plane is officially crashing.

"Out of control," I whisper. "Death."

Later, armed with a Bloody Mary to loosen my tongue, I'm getting to know my blond neighbour. He has the textbook surfer chic about him. Just-out-of-bed hairstyle, a terracotta shirt that has the top two buttons undone to show off a perfect, bronzed, hairless chest. His voice oozes like thick honey in an accent that might be Tennessee or Alabama.

We talk about San Francisco. I lie and say I'm going to visit friends in Sausalito because although I've never been, I've seen pictures and it looks like the sort of place I would've enjoyed visiting when I stayed in Scotland. It reminds me of

Inverkip, but with more money. He tells me he's going for a job interview with Industrial Light & Magic, but for all I know, he could be lying too. Whether he is or he isn't, he's sitting in Business Class so he must be at least semi-successful. Or bumped up from Coach. Whatever. I think he's pretty cool and I pick up the vibe that he's into me because he's sending me all these signals, talking with his hands, trying to make jokes. So I give him signals back, playing with my hair, and twisting myself in my seat so I'm about three-quarters facing him, and we continue flirting while the sun passes by my window and that's when my hand accidentally but not really touches his knee.

"...so my mom thinks I should be able to find graphics work back in New Orleans but, you know, I wanna see some of the country while I'm still young. It's a big country, you know? All my friends at college..."

Everything he's saying, whether intentionally or otherwise, is reminding me of his age and he's drinking Coke, and suddenly he looks about nineteen and I become very conscious that I'm forty-three. I remember Dante. Somewhat latterly, I remember Adam. I feel sick with myself. I withdraw my hand. I want to be a good mother.

We don't say too much to each other after that. In a way, the embarrassment is good because it gives me something to obsess over rather than work myself up into a frenzy about the inevitable landing. Of course, the natural line of logic from that is to contemplate the possibility that my fear of flying could be overcome if I flirted with the boy in the seat next to me every time I stepped onto a plane.

I'm on my second Bloody Mary of the flight, maybe my fourth or fifth of the day, when the blond surfer boy leans across me to look out of the window.

"Lose something?" I ask.

"The sun just went by the window," he says.

"Oh. Okay."

"The sun went by your window shortly after we took off. And then it went by your window again about twenty minutes ago. And again about ten minutes ago."

I stare out of the window and manage to be surprised when I see the sun. The remains of my drink in the little plastic tumbler fills in the rest of the blanks as they seem to slosh over to one side rather than the other.

"We're going in circles," I say. "That's not bad, though, right? That's not necessarily something to be concerned about. Is it? We're not going to crash?"

He shrugs. "Probably not. But this is our fourth circuit. Must be something going on down there."

Before we can speculate further or grab a stewardess to quiz, there's a ping, and the captain makes an announcement. The Surfer Dude and I both look up as if the sound's coming from the overhead buckets.

"Ladies and Gentlemen," he says, "the more chronologically-aware amongst you may have noticed we should be landing round about now."

I check my watch. He's right.

He goes on, "We've been in a holding pattern over San Francisco thanks to a disabled aircraft on the runway. Now, there's absolutely nothing to worry about, folks, because we're not ready to run out of fuel any time soon but we've done about all the holding we can do, and we really need to be setting down soon. Our usual back-ups of San Jose and Oakland are currently running full to capacity, so I'm sorry to tell you all that we'll be detouring north this afternoon to our third alternate at Klamath Falls. I'll be back when I have more details of transfers but in the meantime, please accept my apologies for this inconvenience, sit back and relax and try to enjoy the rest of the flight."

"Sonofabitch," the blond surfer boy mutters.

"What Falls?" I say. "I've no idea where that is."

"Southern Oregon."

"But they can't. I have a connection at four o'clock," I say, like he can do anything about it. "For fuck's sake, they can't do this! I'm supposed to be on a flight to London in an hour and a half!"

He smiles and shakes his head, and I know what he's going to say before he opens his mouth. He seems to know that I know but that only makes him take greater relish as he says, "That's so not going to happen."

iv

The drive to the meeting had left me with no trust in my GPS, and the meeting itself had just made me feel even more isolated, so I decided to drive back home by my wits and sign-reading skills. I wasn't entirely surprised when I found myself heading west into Westwood on Santa Monica Boulevard; a long way for a shortcut even by my standards. Deciding that I could do with some time staring out into the Pacific, I pretended this had been my intention all along and gave the Merc some more gas. I'd travelled another block when the phone rang, and because I knew who it was and why they were calling, my newly established sense of drive and purpose evaporated. My foot rose from the gas.

"Good lunch?" Baby asked. This was her greeting.

"Not really. It was odd. I guess I'm just in an odd mood. I dunno."

"Let me guess. Lobster spaghetti?"

"Spot on."

"Great," she said with a sigh. "He'll be gassy as hell all afternoon. Anyway. I have news regarding your predicament. Are we still talking hypothetically here?"

"For the moment, yes."

"Okay, well, if you'd really wanted to, you could've been on a flight right this second, arriving in Heathrow in time for breakfast tomorrow and then a transfer would've got you back in Glasgow in time for lunch."

"And assuming I can't get my hands on a time machine?"

"Well, there's one at round about ten o'clock tonight on another of our partner carriers, but if that's too much of a rush for you, you're probably best with the same flight around noon tomorrow. You're red-eying all the way, but if it was me, I'd want as much time as possible on the other end to adjust. If you leave tonight, you'll get a sleep on the plane and then have twenty-four hours to recover."

It sounded sensible, and it would give me some time with Adam before the funeral to be a good, comforting mother. Conversely, the idea of spending a day in the knowledge that Helen and Raymond and all the others would be nearby didn't exactly thrill me.

"So, the very latest, I guess, would be noon Sunday?"

Baby said nothing and I imagined her confused, trying to work out why I would possibly want to cut it so fine. Eventually, she said, "Well, I guess, but you'd better hope the funeral's not in the morning because you could still be waiting for your luggage."

"I think it's in the afternoon."

"Really? Because you weren't specific."

"Wasn't I?" I knew for a fact I hadn't been. I had no idea why I was lying.

Another long pause. "No." Another one. Shorter this time. "Look, either way, you're going to be fucked. If I were you, I'd be on that flight this evening. At the very, very latest, noon tomorrow."

"Just to confirm, then," I said, nodding and trying to sound like I was writing this down, "so that's ten o'clock this evening, noon tomorrow, ten tomorrow, noon Sunday."

"Angela. Sweetheart. I'm going compromise my ruthless efficiency with your unbearable procrastination and just put you on the goddamn flight at noon tomorrow. There. It's decided. Okay?"

I opened my mouth to protest but gave up before the merest squeak left me.

"Okay?" She sounded determined, a little annoyed and no doubt keen to draw a line under this so she could move on to whatever other fires she had burning on her desk. "Noon tomorrow? It's no good nodding. I need you to say it."

"Okay, fine," I conceded. "Noon tomorrow."

Half an hour after we hung up, I stood out at the end of Santa Monica pier and watched the swells and crests of the bluest ocean as it shifted beneath a clear blue sky. As beautiful as it looked, today it seemed superficial, and the lack of any other colour frustrated me until I had to turn away and walk back to the car.

I became aware that every second as it thundered by and every step I placed on the wooden boards took me closer to Adam, closer to the funeral, closer to forcing myself onto another couple of flights, with the prospect of getting on two more a few days later to look forward to.

The route back took me past a row of black cannons that pointed out to the Pacific. Even though they were facing in the opposite direction from home, a vague curiosity made me go over and peer inside one, thinking that if they were still operational, maybe I could fire myself home to avoid the flight. Sadly, though, the cannon had been packed with metal so that it was only a foot deep or so. The reason for choking it up, I decided, was to prevent people like me from putting their bizarre, imaginary travel plans into action.

Something about the cannon did surprise me, however; specifically, something inside it. Leaning against the packed in metal, there sat an orange and blue can, instantly familiar yet unimaginably alien in this part of the world. Disregarding all sense of hygiene and sanity, I reached in and plucked it out.

It was a retro can of Irn Bru, one I remembered from the 90s. It was an American can of Irn Bru, it had been labelled as a Fruit Flavored Punch Drink, but it still sported the logo of the dancing dude in the white shorts, and it bore the Glasgow address. It was the real deal. My heart bounced as adrenaline pulsed through me and my mouth dried up. I contemplated the odds. It had to be a sign. What other reason could there have been to drive miles out of my way to peer inside this particular dysfunctional cannon? It was a sign.

This time next week, I told myself while I looked at this piece of home in my hand, either I would be back in LA, finishing off the work on the summer schedule, or I'd be mangled in a wreckage somewhere. Either way, it would all be over, and that would just have to be good enough for the time being.

Back in the car and halfway back to Culver City, I realised I still had the can with me.

$$5$$

Although the landing is smooth and turbulence-free, on a very fundamental level it still carries that familiar flavour of being out of control and death. I try to keep it swallowed down and contained, but I still do my best to tear my chair to pieces. Blond surfer boy has the wisdom to keep his mouth shut this time.

Later, after we disembark, I learn from local tourism adverts that Klamath Falls—Oregon's City of Sunshine, no less—sits about twenty miles north of the border with California. The airport serves as a base for a military unit whose name I forget, but there are enough private and commercial planes scattered about, so it doesn't feel like we've landed in the middle of Area 51. The buildings that make up the airport must have less square feet than one level of a medium-sized car park at LAX. It really is that small. However, the saddest thing about Klamath Falls is that it reminds me of home. It's set amongst achingly beautiful, mountainous scenery and with such a low ceiling of cloud. It even has the good grace to have its own loch.

I'm about sixth in a queue waiting to speak to an airline rep when my phone lights up and vibrates in my hand. Baby's details appear on the display. I feel so stressed that even though she's in a far better position to get me moving, I don't particularly want to speak to her right now; almost as much as I know I have to. As though I'm pulling off a plaster, I answer before the phone buzzes for a second time.

"How's Oregon?" she asks, again dispensing with a more formal greeting.

"That's not funny."

The angry businesswoman at the front of the queue is so red there are actually hints of black in her complexion as she bellows at the rep, "What kind of incident? What does that even mean? Incident?"

"Aw, come on, it's a little amusing. Are you still at the airport?"

"I'm not shouting!" Angry Lady shouts.

I put a finger in my ear. It doesn't really help. I see Blond Surfer Boy wander through the arrivals lounge. I feel a bit sorry for him—and wonder if he is that young after all—but need to keep focussed so I look at a new scratch that's appeared on my Louis Vuitton luggage.

"Aye. I'm waiting to speak to the rep about getting...somewhere."

"Yeah, well, don't give yourself a heart attack. You're not going anywhere."

"What? Why not?"

"Where the hell am I?" Angry Lady demands.

"Nothing's getting in or out of San Francisco, sweetheart. It's shut down."

I'm about to ask why when I decide it doesn't matter. I run a hand through my hair. "Great," I say. "Where does that leave us?"

"Well, ideally, it means you should've listened to me and got the Friday flight. Pragmatically, it means you should get yourself over to the Avis desk and hire a car. You've got a long drive ahead of you."

I scrunch up my face and shake my head. I can feel the blood begin to bubble round my body.

"Seriously? You want me to drive to San Francisco?" I have no idea of the precise distance, but from the map that's on the wall behind the rep's desk, it looks a good four or five hundred miles.

"No. Like I told you, San Francisco's shut. I want you to drive to Portland."

That looks a bit better, but there's not much in it. More than that, though, there's a question I want to ask with an answer I'm not sure I want to hear. I ask it anyway.

"Baby, am I going to make it back on time? Is that even possible?"

She hums for a moment as though she doesn't want to commit herself one way or the other. "It's not Monday yet. Jesus, it's not even Sunday yet."

"Do you believe in fate, Baby?"

"I believe in regularly scheduled flights."

I nod impatiently at her flippancy while the queue takes a step forward and the beetroot lady storms away.

"But do you know what I mean? It's like something's conspiring against me. Something doesn't want me to get to Glasgow."

"Sweetheart, the only thing that doesn't want you to get to Glasgow is you. If you don't want to go, fine. Drive all the way back to LA if you so desire. It makes absolutely no difference to me one way or the other. If you want to go—"

"I want to be a good mother."

"—then I suggest you haul your ass to Avis before everything with four wheels is taken. Tomorrow morning, you'll fly to JFK, and if you have one fucking ounce of luck at all, you'll make a connection that'll take you direct into Glasgow for seven on Monday morning and then I can close this file and die a happy woman."

Half an hour later, a thin woman with impeccable make-up at the Avis desk gives me the documents for a Durango along with a map that has all the charm and detail of a roadside diner placemat. When I ask, she tells me I should be in Portland in five-and-a-half hours depending on traffic, which is what Baby reckoned before we hung up on each other. The angry businesswoman from earlier is served after me, and when I see that her complexion has returned to a more healthy pink, I offer her a smile.

"Planes," I say, rolling my eyes.

"Fucking planes," the pink lady says.

The car turns out to be pretty comfortable, but it's too long and wide for my tastes, and it just contributes to the sensation of isolation I've been experiencing for the last few days.

"What am I doing?" I murmur to myself as I turn the key. I don't expect it to start. In fact, based on the way my day's going, I half-expect it to blow up, so it's something of a surprise when the engine coughs into life first time. If anything, it makes me more suspicious.

The guy on the barrier at the exit to the lot checks my paperwork. He looks as old and as weathered as the faded high-visibility jacket he wears. He has life experiences, I'm sure. He should be whittling wooden animals from fallen trees and selling them from a stall at the side of the highway. Or something like that, anyway.

"What've ye got?" he asks, his eyes flicking between me and the back seat.

I blink rapidly as I try to process the words I'm sure I heard. "Excuse me?"

"Where—are—you—going?" he repeats as though he's talking to a confused child.

"Portland," I say absently, still a little stunned. "I'm going to Portland."

"Take it tae number five," he says.

"I'm sorry, sir," I say, "but I'm having a real problem tuning in to your accent."

He sighs and hands me another map. "Interstate Five."

The barrier rises, and for whatever reason, I'm very nervous as I edge through and onto the roads of Klamath Falls.

"What am I doing?" I mutter.

I don't think I know anymore.

V

That night, I had another dream about earthquakes, and although it ended up being different from the others, it started in the same mundane, surreal territory as all the others. This time, I found myself in a meeting in an old-fashioned board room on the fiftieth floor of a hotel in Kuala Lumpur; a place I had never visited and wouldn't have thought I could've recognised supposing my life depended on it, but dreams have their own rules. The room was very humid. That may have been what made me associate it with the Far East. So the meeting was long and boring and pretty much impossible to differentiate from real life except the massive table we all sat around came up to just below my shoulders. Everyone else at the meeting—people I took to be Michael's bosses—sat at a normal level with their hands clasped in front of them, looking very somber. After a while, I became conscious that I hadn't contributed anything so far to the discussion and perhaps because everyone else could only see my head and face, I was terrified I was going to fall asleep and slip under the table. So there I was, dreaming about struggling to stay awake. The guy across from me blethered on about some correlation he'd found between Nielsen ratings and the colour of font used in a show's title card. The guy next to him—younger, buff, with an Ashton Kutcher vibe and a pierced eyebrow—kept winking at me through an otherwise blank expression and even though the table stretched out twenty feet between us, he was playing footsie with me. My face contorted goofily as my eyebrows stretched halfway up my forehead in an attempt to prop my eyes open. The guy's ratings talk had moved on to observe that five in the morning was begging to become the new prime time when the tremor started in the floor, and for a while, it felt like nothing more than a subway train running beneath the building. No one appeared overly concerned, so I chose not to worry, but before long, the tremor increased until pens and paper started to shimmy across the table, and a plastic cup of water—that I would've sworn hadn't existed until that moment—tipped over. Then, my pen raised off the table and floated at eye level, suspended by the force of its own vibration, and the tremor roared and screamed, as though a monster had woken up. The talking guy swiftly adjourned the meeting and ran out of the room, the footsie guy, and all the others close on his heels, and as soon as they left, the doors disappeared with them. So that left me alone in the room, which had become a cell, with every wall a window and no obvious way in or out. Well, in my dream, that woke me up a bit. Finally deciding to panic, I ran over to the nearest window and pounded my fists against the glass because on some level I was aware I was dreaming and if I could smash the glass, I could jump out, and I knew I'd wake up. Fifty floors below, the street was chaotic. A crack chased cars towards a locked intersection, ridging up the road like a scar, throwing pedestrians off their feet and into buildings where they smashed and crumpled and fell. The sky, of course, turned red, clouds became balls of fire as lava oozed like blood from the wound on the street. The building swayed, and ceiling tiles rained down. Swarms of flies—the size of Coke cans, eyes like quarters—dive-bombed into the window, turning to bloody ash as soon as they made contact with the glass and once they evaporated, they left dents that told me they'd break through eventually and when they did, I'd drown in them. From somewhere, I heard someone remark that the Blockbuster down the street had rented out all its zombie movies. I saw a reflection of a man, yellow and gaunt with eyes so deeply set in his head, they were just black holes. Behind him, I saw a woman in a fur coat except her face was pixilated and anonymous. When I looked behind me, they were nowhere to be seen, and I was still alone. Still, the sky burned and the ground melted. The building—which had become the only one left standing because all the others had capsized—bucked and pitched and rolled like a buoy in the ocean and I felt I was surfing on the floor to keep my balance. Fire began to rain down in the room, and the glass and the floor began to crumble, pushing me to the centre of the room, looking for the massive table that no longer existed and

I remembered thinking if I couldn't get close enough to the window to throw myself out, how was I going to wake myself up. For the first time, I knew this wasn't really an earthquake. I knew I was witnessing the end of the world.

149

6

It's approaching ten o'clock when I walk into the Ramada Portland Airport after dropping the car off at Avis. I'm glad to see the back of it, even though that means hauling my poor Louis Vuitton onto a shuttle bus. During the six-hour drive, the Durango had come to represent a state of limbo and no matter how many times I told myself I was doing something positive and that these were miles being travelled towards a goal, that I was 300 miles closer to doing the right thing and being a good mother, it didn't stick. The car was a bubble. Time stood still inside the bubble. Outside, the world was flat and ordinary, and while the road rumbled below at a steady 65, everything else might as well have been projected on a screen. I just wanted to get to where I needed to get, go to my room, go to bed and wake up when it would be morning.

But I don't go to the room once I've checked in. Instead, I drag my luggage with me to the bar and practically throw myself on to a stool. My neighbours are business types, lots of suits, mostly male, and they don't acknowledge my arrival. I could be anyone. I could be anywhere.

The hunky young bartender mixes me a Bloody Mary as I contemplate whether I was over the limit when I drove up from Wichita Falls or whatever it was called. My inability to remember the town's name moves me to wonder if it's really a question of how much I was over the limit.

I'm on my second drink, thinking about ordering some sushi or something with my third drink when I sense someone sit on the stool next to me. It's testament to how quickly airport hotels drain all the enthusiasm and life from its customers when I don't look at my new neighbour, and I behave in the exact same, cocooned way as my businessmen colleagues did when I turned up. Motivated by a need to differentiate myself from them rather than any genuine curiosity or desire to appear friendly, I twist myself round to check it out.

We stare at each other for a little while, and she stutters—thrown from her train of thought—as she orders a gin and tonic but after the bartender prepares her drink she says, "Fucking planes," to me, and we start to laugh.

"San Francisco," I say.

"Klamath Falls," the pink lady says. "This time tomorrow, we'll be in Seattle."

I groan. "I hope not."

"Where should you be right now?"

"God, there's a question." It's quite odd to be having this conversation within a minute of her arriving, but then it seemed more odd to leave it at that. Pointlessly, I look at my watch. "Technically, I suppose I should be in London. Either that, I should be in LA."

"Didn't you come from LA?"

It seemed so long ago. Was that really today? Was it just twelve hours ago that a slightly overweight, non-talkative, disinterested Hispanic driver named Jorge picked me up? Full of shame, I think of Dante and wonder if he's found the note yet.

"You know," I say eventually, "this is all pretty much Jethro Tull's fault."

"If I had a nickel..." pink lady murmurs. She's served her drink and raises it to me. "Cheers," she says, and we clink glasses.

"What about you? Where should you be?"

The smile that had been on her face since we started

talking falls and I'm reminded of how she looked when she was Angry Lady, and she was shouting at the airline reps.

"Know what? I think I'll know when I get there. It hasn't happened yet."

"Okay. Well, that's quite mysterious."

And then she's smiling again, and she cocks her head in a way that says, Darling, you don't know the half of it, before taking a generous sip of her drink.

When she offers nothing more, I take a gamble with her mood and try to prompt her further by saying, "I guess I thought I'd be the only person who'd try to fly to San Francisco, miss and then drive away from it."

"When you don't have a purpose, it's kinda hard to know where you're supposed to be. What's your purpose?"

It's beyond odd. It makes oddness look quite normal by comparison, but it's been such a long, stupid day, any barriers I should be erecting at this point are too slow and ineffective, and I'm answering before I'm fully aware of doing so.

"I need to get across the Atlantic. My ex-husband died. I'm going back to Scotland for his funeral."

"You have a funereal look about you. But if you don't mind me saying, that's not your purpose. That's your reaction to something. That's passive. A purpose is active."

I think for a second then nod. "No, you're absolutely right. I'm not going back for him. If he had any sway on my life whatsoever, he wouldn't be an ex-husband, now would he? I need to go back for my son. I need to make him feel better."

It's her turn to nod, but she does so solemnly as she says, "You're a good mom."

The barriers, somewhat belatedly, shoot up. I feel my posture shrink into myself. I face more toward the bar than to my neighbour. A chill starts in my heart and pumps round me until I shiver like I'm sitting under the air-con. The most disconcerting thing, though, is I don't think I've properly considered what it takes to be a good mother. I've convinced myself that I want to be one, but I have no idea what that means, if I am one already, if I even have the capacity within myself to become one, if I even want to. Suddenly, hearing a stranger make the observation has made the thing that kept me company for six hours on the road feel ridiculous and false. If we'd had this exchange back in Klamath Falls, I might have driven south instead.

"I'm sorry," the pink lady says. "I have an uncontrollable habit to say the most inappropriate things to perfect strangers. You don't need to comment on that. You shouldn't comment on that. I don't know you. You don't know me. It's none of my business."

I concoct a smile from somewhere. "It's just—"

She holds up her hands, shushing me. "Forget it. Let me buy you a drink, and then I'll leave you to your evening."

We share an awkward silence while she tries to attract the bartender's attention. When she does, she's well-versed in bar sign language and gives him the signal by tapping the empty air above my glass.

"So where are you heading really?" I ask, trying to lighten the mood and also because it strikes me as being improper to say thanks, that doing so would be the equivalent of saying there was no need for her to apologise.

She screws up her face like we've already covered this, pushes a few single bills across the bar and stands up. "I don't know," she says. "But wherever it is, there's no going back now."

vi

The memory of the dream stayed with me long into the day, so strong that at several points I could think of nothing else— not my travel plans, not my work, not the fact Dante still hadn't come home—and even when it wasn't on my mind, I had a hum or a vibration in my gut that made me more reluctant to fly and convinced it was only a matter of time before the dream came true.

Still, my choice of things to do felt limited. I could either work or pack, and I felt very far away from being in the right place creatively to do any work. My mind simply couldn't focus in that direction. So by mid-afternoon, with the blinds in the house still closed, I wandered from one monochrome room to the next, collecting items I knew I would never wear, moving them from one place to the next, reminding myself I'd need something black. It surprised me to find that the closest thing I had was a slate grey cocktail dress I absolutely adored but had always associated with a movie premiere Dante and I attended last summer. I wasn't sure I wanted to associate it with a funeral. I wasn't sure I wanted to associate it with Dante.

Dante's whereabouts were still a mystery but, again, felt limited. He wasn't at home. He didn't have a job so couldn't very well be at work. He had to be somewhere. He had to be doing something. I'd phoned a couple of mutual friends, warning them that I might be out of town for a few days next week in case they needed to get a hold of me and hoping one of them would mention Dante or his current locale without me having to shame myself by asking. Such intelligence didn't materialize, and I ended up spending a few hours talking about my ex-husband's funeral with people I hadn't really wanted to talk to in the first place.

So I still lacked any real sense of the conclusion I reckoned I needed before I'd be able to train my focus elsewhere. Baby had proved the journey could be made. Michael's ambivalence told me it should. I figured I needed five minutes with Dante before I knew if it would.

It might have been around four o'clock when I didn't know what else to do, so I decided to write Dante a letter. I'd never been that big a letter writer, but there have been times in my life when it simply seemed the thing to do, even if I found the whole process tiring and awkward. A few years ago, when Adam and I first got back in touch, he wrote to me, and it was such a sweet, brave thing to do, I tried to write him back. The words didn't come to me, and I couldn't match Adam's honesty, and the whole business seemed so alien and false. As a cop-out, I thought I could substitute a few thousand words with some photos, and that was when I realised I didn't have any. The last twelve years and the people I'd shared them with hadn't been recorded. There was absolutely nothing to send. So I had to force more of the letter out, all the while totally spooked by the absence of photographs and that afternoon, as I tried to write a letter to Dante, I felt the same. Again, I hoped to find a substitute—a non-photographic substitute—that would come to my rescue and fill in some of the blanks for me. Nothing did.

So, it took a while. After I was done, I packed the cocktail dress anyway.

7

ut of control. Death. Oh, whatever.

A carrier I hadn't heard of before today is charged with delivering me safely to New York and to be fair, for a Mom and Pop airline, they give the impression they've done this sort of thing before, and for the most part, it all goes according to plan.

My favourite part of the flight—other than the fact that it didn't explode shortly after take-off—is that it has a screen that shows a map of the arcing route across country from PDX to JFK with a little logo of the plane showing where we are in real time. There's also some dull information about airspeed and outside temperature, but it's the wee graphic of the plane that really holds my attention. Strangely, focussing on the plane makes me forget I'm flying or at least allows my attention to wander away from the fact. The little graphic is going too slow to crash, it will never lose all power in three of its engines, and the pilot and crew of the little graphic won't have had the fish and collapse with food poisoning.

My least favourite part of the flight is there's no Business Class. There's Coach and Coach Plus. With nothing obvious to physically show where one starts and the other finishes, the only benefits of Coach Plus appear to be a complimentary breakfast bagel (sausage or jelly), a copy of USA Today (does anyone actually pay money for this newspaper?) and maybe an extra inch of leg room. All other food and drink must be purchased, which frankly sucks ass. I must be cheaper than I think because this is enough to keep me off the Bloody Marys and I have to nurse a strangely persistent hangover with Vanquish and mineral water. I'd give my every last cent for one full, chilled can of that Fruit Flavoured Punch drink I found in Santa Monica.

The fax confirmation Baby sent through to me last night is folded up in my inside jacket pocket. According to this, and to the screen showing the flight progress, I'll get into JFK a couple of hours from now at four in the afternoon where I'll have almost three full hours of a buffer before the Glasgow flight departs. From there, Coach Plus will be made to feel like my own personal Lear Jet as the Glasgow leg of the trip will be the one-size-fits-all hell that is Chartered, but all going well should deliver me at around seven o'clock tomorrow morning. Give me an hour to get through Customs and baggage reclaim and another hour in a taxi and I should be with Adam at nine. Ten at the latest. Surely nothing can go wrong now.

I smile and then I crack, and start laughing. Luckily, there's no one in the seat next to me, and I'm able to quickly disguise the laughter as a half-sneeze, half-cough with no embarrassment but then my hands clutch on to my cramping stomach.

Adam.

I realise I haven't spoken to him since—what was it—Wednesday. He doesn't know I'm on my way. I don't have his number on my mobile. The aftertaste of laughter is quickly washed away by a panic that dashes through me.

Lying on grass. Floating on the ocean. Deep breaths.

It's the twenty-first century. How hard can it be to track someone down? Christ, Baby could probably do it in her sleep. In any event, there's nothing I can do about it right now, but I make a note to do something to sort it all out while i'm waiting on my connection.

I'm proud of myself. Not even the sudden appearance of a minor dilemma is enough to push me from my happy cloud, and when I discover that the hangover is starting to fade, I'm pleased but not wholly surprised. Today, I promise myself, is when everything falls into place.

What does surprise me is the little plane icon on the TV screen because rather than remaining fixed on the route line, it's now jumping from one location to the next like a moth burning its feet on the screen. It places me in Miami, Washington DC, Kansas, Anchorage, San Diego, the Caribbean, everywhere it seems except New York. I know it's just a glitch. I know it's the same sort of thing that happened to my GPS during the drive to Oskar, but it's very disconcerting and puts me on alert, makes me jittery. Now, the slightest change in pitch in the plane's engines is a failing engine, every rattle in the overhead buckets is a bomb and all the good, positive work I feel I've done on the flight so far is unravelled and I have to watch the screen and the frantic plane graphic because if I look away, I'll imagine it getting worse and when it does get worse, I realise it's actually different from the GPS in the car because here, there's no button to turn it off.

vii

Dante came home at around eight that evening. If he said hello when he walked in, I didn't hear it, and then he disappeared into the bathroom and stayed there for so long, I began to think I'd imagined him or he'd been a ghost floating along the hall. When he came out, he was still wearing his shades and whatever he'd been doing in the bathroom hadn't required a flush. I couldn't imagine. I didn't want to know.

"Shall we go eat?" he asked. I'd almost forgotten the hint of French in his accent. Hunger and a brief flash of desire both trumped anger, so I agreed.

We ended up in an Italian restaurant on Venice Boulevard, not too far from home. Dante decided he'd drive but whatever substances he had coursing through his system meant he drove so slowly, we were only marginally quicker than walking.

It must've been around nine thirty when we sat at a table at the window. He ordered seafood pizza. I couldn't be bothered reading the menu—and now we were here, and I had time to think about it, I felt too sick to eat anyway—so I ordered the same. He hadn't removed his shades at this point, and I played with the idea of pointing this out to him because I suspected he might have been wondering why everything was so dark. I left him be because they probably hid a million sins and the flash of desire returned to point out how very moody and sexy he looked. When the pizza arrived, I'd decided on which topic I wanted to raise first. His whereabouts for the last couple of days could wait. I needed my five minutes to talk about my plans and, in any event, the importance of his disappearance had subsided since he'd come back.

"I'm going to Scotland," I said it in a rush.

"Where? Why?"

"There's a funeral I need to go to," I explained. And then, because I wasn't sure he picked it up the first time, I repeated, "In Scotland."

"Who died?"

"You don't know him."

"Him?"

"It was my ex-husband."

"Scotland's...far?"

I scratched my head, eventually nodded when he looked to be waiting on a response.

"How long will you be?"

"I'm not sure. A few days."

"A few days?" He slammed his hands down on the table, making me flinch and the cutlery hop on the table.

"I should be back before Thursday," I said, unsure if that was likely.

"That's a week."

"Just about, yes."

"What am I meant to do?"

"Well, fucking hell, Dante, I dunno. How about whatever you've been up to for the last few days?"

I didn't want to go down this road. I wanted to focus on the trip. The disappearance, I'd pretended to myself, could wait until I got back.

"I'm here, aren't I?" he said.

"Almost." There was a pause, and I couldn't work a way out, so I said, "Do you need money? Is that why you came back? Is that why you want me to stay?"

He ignored me. "Where are you going?"

"I told you. Scotland."

"Yeah, but I thought you were afraid of flying?"

"I am. I'm terrified."

"Then why are you going?"

"Because," I snapped. I calmed before I continued, "it's my ex-husband's funeral."

"Well, Angela. Why would you go to your ex-husband's funeral? Isn't that weird?"

"I'm not going for him. I'm going for my son. I'm going so I can be there for Adam."

He produced a crooked Marlboro Light from a pocket and slotted it into the corner of his mouth. Thankfully, he couldn't magic up a lighter, so he removed the cigarette and tapped it on the white tablecloth until little splinters of tobacco fell out.

"Do you not want me to go?" I asked.

He didn't say anything.

"Do you need me to stay? Do you think I shouldn't go?"

"How old is Adam?" he asked. It surprised me to feel stung a little by this. I didn't like him saying my son's name.

"He'll be...twenty-six."

Dante smiled. "He's the same age as me."

"Actually he's a few months older than you. But yes. More or less."

"Well," he said, still smiling. "I guess my question is this. Would you travel halfway round the world to be there for me?"

I looked at the reflection of myself in his shades. There were two of me, identical in every way. Still looking good for my age, still easily mistaken for being in my thirties, still with that perfectly straight bob and the beauty spot that really couldn't have been closer to Marilyn Monroe's if it tried, looking better for having had some sleep, head perfectly still. But I thought that despite the identical nature of these images, it was a classic devil and angel situation. Bad Angela. Good Angela. And there I was, facing the two of them, sitting in between, trying to work out the right thing to say, hoping I'd be able to stick to my guns, whatever I decided. I looked back and forth between the clones and hoped one would give me a sign. No sign came. There was only an answer.

"No," one of them said. "I don't think I would."

Dante didn't look sad or angry or happy or relieved or anything, really. He put his cigarette back in his pocket, nodded like he had expected my reply and then stared at his seafood pizza that already looked cold and congealed. I don't know what he saw on his plate that was so interesting, but whatever it was, it held his attention for a very long time.

8

JFK is a horrible place but it's such a novel feeling to be where I'm scheduled to be that it's all I can do not to drop to my knees and kiss the manky floor in the arrivals hall. I'm getting there. Slowly but surely. I pick up my luggage and drag it behind me as if it's an uncooperative child as I march through arrivals.

When I'm on the AirTrain—crowded, hot, smelly—waiting to be taken to the next terminal, I switch on my cell. There are five missed calls, all number withheld, but no messages. Probably because he's on my mind, I decide it has to be Adam. There's a chance it could be Dante, I suppose, but chatting on the phone was never really his style. No, it had to be Adam. He's managed to track me down. Maybe he got my number from Dante.

So I phone Baby, only realising when it starts to ring that it's Sunday and it's three hours earlier back in California. Despite this, she answers just as the AirTrain pulls away.

"Let me guess. Diverted to Beirut?" This is her greeting.

"It's hard to tell."

"So you're there, you're on time?"

"Yes. I've got some time to kill but terrorist attacks and natural disasters notwithstanding, it's looking good for a seven o'clock departure."

"Good. So what can I do for you? Or rather, what can I do for you now?"

So I explain about contacting Adam. I imagine her shaking her head on the other end of the phone. I imagine her pinching the bridge of her nose. I imagine her lighting up a fresh cigarette with the butt of an old one.

"I'll see what I can do," she says.

I want to avoid even the slightest chance of anything going wrong, so when I arrive at the terminal, I check in immediately, shuffle through security, find a quiet corner of the departure lounge close to where I expect the gate to be when it's eventually announced, and I even avoid the bar.

The area where I sit has a massive window that looks out on to the green marshland of Jamaica Bay. It's still afternoon, but the spring sun is made to look lower than it is thanks to the distant skyline of Manhattan. It's a gorgeous pink evening. High-level clouds are illuminated in ambers and crimsons, wisps of paint against the blue.

I stand to get a better view because it really is an astonishing sight and it inspires me to think back to the last time I did this; the last time I just took a moment. The hour or two I have to wait now feels like an eternity, and I imagine the colours I'll see during that time as the westbound sun does its best to drain everything to black. It makes me think of chasing the sun, of following it as it makes its journey and holds pieces of the world in a perpetual sunset because it would be good to keep it looking as beautiful as it does right now.

From the marshland a group of large birds—herons, perhaps, or storks—emerge from the long grass and seem to share my idea, and they rise towards the clouds, their long necks stretching out, giving them the appearance of distant planes and I watch them, heading west, maybe appalled by my presence, maybe scared off by me or maybe reminding me that it's the twenty-first century and anything is possible, and it's good to have time to think. It's never too late to do the right thing. One more flight, I realise. Another few hours. I stand and watch and hold my stomach.

Eventually, long after the birds have shrunk to dots and

disappeared, my phone lights up and vibrates in my hand. It keeps on ringing then stops and then seconds later, it starts again. I look down at the phone, not deliberately meaning to read the display, but it's impossible to avoid it as my finger reaches out to turn the phone off.

Cannons. The sun. Storks. All pointing back west. All pointing back to LA.

viii

While Friday ticked into Saturday, I listened to Dante breathing as he slept, snoring lightly while he lay naked next to me. His skin glowed with an orange highlight of sweat thanks to the streetlights outside, his shades had been torn off and thrown on the floor. I kinda wished he still had them on.

I couldn't sleep, but it wasn't because I was stressed by any complications. There were no obstacles anymore; no one left to speak to. The fact that I could disappear to the other side of the world for a week and only need to speak to a couple of people truly depressed me.

The idea of getting on a plane made me shiver and toss my head until the idea disappeared, but even that couldn't be responsible for keeping me awake. I'd flown before. Six months ago, I had flown back and forth between Miami and LA twice a week for a month. I hated every minute of it, and for those four weeks even the sound of a plane flying overhead would shred my nerves but I got through it, and I always managed to sleep.

I got out of bed and put some clothes on. Not outdoor clothes, just panties, and a baggy Peanuts t-shirt. For a while, I stood at the sink under the kitchen window and let a glass fill and then overfill with cold water. I opened the blinds, releasing more streetlight into the room. Outside, the city was quiet, and it was impossible to tell if the rush I could hear was traffic on the distant freeway or just blood pressure hissing in my ears.

On the way back to bed, I noticed the envelope I'd left on the dresser in case Dante hadn't come back in time. As hard as I tried, I could remember very little of its contents, so I lifted the unsealed envelope and took out the letter. I checked over my shoulder to make sure he didn't wake, but even if he had, I didn't expect him to be too interested.

Dante, I'd written, I'm going away for a few days, and when I come back, I don't want you to be here. Take whatever you want. I don't care. Just go. Don't come back.

The letter was short, so I had time to read it several times. It took no effort to recreate the emotions I felt during its creation. They were feelings I had felt for most of the relationship. It couldn't last. I wasn't sure I even wanted it to last. He'd grow bored. Maybe he was always bored. What was certain was I knew my five minutes with him—the five minutes I'd been so desperate to have—had been a bust. Nothing he could have said stood any chance of making up my mind, and I realised his involvement wasn't specifically what I needed. I needed five minutes with anyone who'd listen. I needed five minutes with anyone who might want me to stay.

At some point, I stopped being a person reading a letter and became a person just holding a piece of paper, but when it came to putting it back in the envelope, it felt the way I did when I stood at the gate, waiting to board a plane. My palms clammed up. My heart began to race. I became short of breath. I felt my knuckles tense around the page. The edges of my vision started to crackle.

I took deep lungfuls of air. Closed my eyes. Concentrated on slowing my pulse.

Eating an apple. Reading a book.

The fear of flying. Was that what it was? Was that what it ever was? Or was it the fear of flight? The fear of landing, perhaps? The fear of change.

Floating on the ocean. Lying on cool grass.

I folded the page over and slid it back in the envelope, and the room spun, and I had to cover my mouth because the noise of my breathing was sure to wake Dante.

It was done. The letter was back, but I decided to

sweeten it a little. I took the money I had in the house—maybe $300 or $400 or so—and put it in the envelope to make it easy for him, to let him know that I knew what this was about for him and I wasn't unreasonable. Then, I unfastened my bracelet and dropped it in too. I didn't expect him to take it, but I felt better for offering something personal to remember me by. I'd had the bracelet for longer than I could remember. I wasn't even sure who'd given it to me or if I'd bought it myself or how long I'd had it, but that bracelet and its little bird charms were part of me. Now it was part of his severance package. It felt like the right thing to do. Even if he held it in his hands and wondered what the fuck it was, even if he eventually pawned it, it didn't matter. I'd done the right thing. Maybe getting rid of birds fastened round other bits of my body was something I should've done a long time ago.

I sealed the envelope and lay it back against the mirror on the dresser, already feeling better, feeling tired. Carefully, I slid back into bed, closed my eyes and waited for a dream about earthquakes, which in the end didn't come.

9

The dream I have during the final flight is of being grounded, on a beach and I think it's St Andrews because I can hear aircraft from RAF Leuchars, but I think on some level I must know that the noise is from the plane I'm on and by extension, I must also have a decent idea that I'm dreaming. I seem to accept it and push it to one side because it continues and I don't wake up.

In the dream, Baby is with me. She's with me, but she's hundreds of yards away down the other end of the deserted beach. The sand is my favourite; wet and solid so it cools my feet but doesn't leave irritating grains between my toes, and that's when I realise I'm barefoot and I'm wearing my little slate grey cocktail dress. I have a niggle I'm still underdressed.

"You're fine," Baby says. When she speaks, it's as though she's standing right beside me. I'm closer to her now and I can see she's dressed up too in a fur coat, which makes sense because there's a chilling wind whipping over from the North Sea. My shoulders are bare and white. I should've had a scarf with me.

I walk towards her. I think she's facing me but it's hard to tell.

"We used to come here," I tell her. "When Adam was wee. We had a caravan up yonder on that hill up there."

The part of me that knows this is a dream also knows we

had a caravan, but it wasn't at St Andrews. We couldn't afford St Andrews. The other part of me tells the first part to shut up.

Baby laughs. "You're funny."

"How?"

"How?" she mimics. "Since when did how mean why?"

I scowl at her and carry on. "He loved his digging, so he did. Wee Adam and his daddy would spend hours on this beach and those rock pools. We thought it was a shame there's nae sandcastle building at the Olympics or oor Adam would be on the podium."

"Uh-huh," Baby says.

"And I longed tae have a dug."

"A dug?"

"Aye, a dug. A collie or a lab. A big friendly beast. Daisy, we'd call it, whether it was a boy or a lassie. It didnae matter. It'd be called Daisy."

The other part of me goes off to check to see if this is true. When it comes back, it shrugs its shoulders. It doesn't know.

"You can't call a male dog Daisy," Baby insists.

"How no? It's a fucking dug. It disnae ken." I look out at the sea which is perfectly flat and still, like a sheet of glass. "We loved this place."

"Is it not a bit late for all this?" Baby asks.

I turn to her and I'm much closer now but I can't make out her face. I get angry; angry that she doesn't have the decency to face me but furious that she chooses to bring this up now and I start to suspect that she isn't Baby at all. I start to suspect that she's actually the part of me that knows this is a dream and just wants to piss on my chips.

"That isnae fair," I tell her. "I'm mourning here."

"It's right, though. And no amount of Scottish countryside or fake Scottish accents or shortbread tins or flying fucking haggis is going to make it otherwise. You've made your decision. You're following the storks."

"Yer saying I made the wrong decision. If yer pert of me, ye had a vote in all this."

"I'm not saying you made the wrong decision. I just want you to live with the decision you made. You've come a long way and then changed your mind. I don't want you to torture yourself anymore by changing it back."

I get even closer to Baby or the Baby imposter. It's no use, though. Her face is still pixilated.

"I wanted tae be a guid mother," I say. "I wanted tae dae the right thing for ma laddie. I think I'm still doing that."

"Hey, if it's any consolation, I agree."

I look down at my feet and watch my toes squish into the sand. It looks so real.

"D'ye think I'll remember this?"

"Which part?"

"The part where I'm sure I'm doing the right thing, even after I wake up?"

"So you know it's a dream, do you?"

"Well, if you ken, ah ken."

Baby laughs. "I think you'll remember. And if you don't, I'll try to remember to tell you once we're back in LA."

"Thanks."

In my hand, I find the old can of Irn Bru, except now it's unopened and has weight as it rolls back and forth in my palm. I imagine it, all ginger and fizzy; a modern day cure-all. If I think hard enough, I can just about remember the taste on my tongue. If it wasn't for the fact I could feel Baby watching me, I might stay in this spot a bit longer. I might have even opened the can and had a wee drink. But I don't. Instead, I let it go. It rolls out of my hand and disappears deep into a bin, becoming lost in chip wrappers and discarded ice cream cones.

I leave Baby after that. I follow the signs pointing west with Daisy the dog at my heels, knowing that somewhere over the horizon there lives silent cannons and exhausted storks, empty envelopes and places to disappear behind sunglasses and closed blinds. I've only taken a few steps when I feel the earthquake coming and I know that when it hits, it's going to be a big one. That's when I wake up.

The Book of Vindication

SECRETS OF THE BURIAL

15

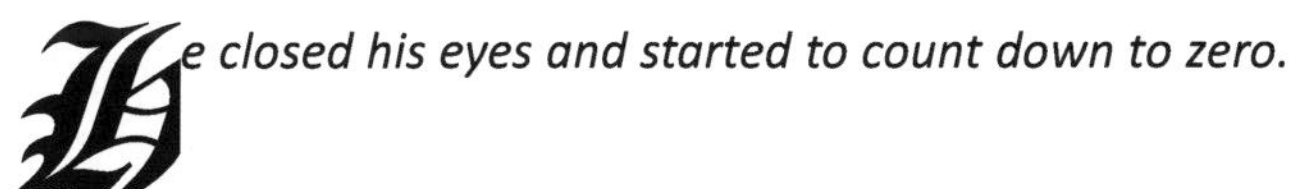

He closed his eyes and started to count down to zero.

14

y mam's a fucking nightmare with that carpet sweeper, so she is.

Huda-huda-huda. Huda-huda-huda. Huda-huda-huda.

It's what wakes me up in the morning. It's the tune that plays after every meal. It's what I hear last thing before lights out.

It's not our caravan, she keeps reminding us, so she's always darting about like a wee pocket dynamo, desperate tae keep the place spick and span. Now, there's keeping something clean, and there's keeping something clean, and then there's keeping something clean, and if it wasnae for the fact she'd scud my jaw, I'd tell her she's spending so much time cleaning, she's forgetting she's supposed tae be on fucking holiday.

"Billy," she snaps at me, slapping my legs. "Billy. Yer feet."

I huff and puff and howk my feet off the floor, planting them beside me on the sofa bunk so I'm lying out on my side. I'm actually comfier now, but I still scowl at the intrusion.

"Shoes," she snaps again, slapping my legs again. "Off the fixtures, if ye please."

I groan, spin so I'm sitting upright and hug my knees, my feet hanging in the air in front ae me. This is definitely the least comfy position, but it lets the sweeper get right intae the nooks and crannies.

Huda-huda-huda. Huda-huda-huda. Huda-huda-huda.

"Right ye are," she says, and I'm allowed tae put my feet back down. "Ken, Billy, yer nothing but a bloody nuisance sitting there with yer face tripping ye. Away out and get some fresh air or something. Away outside and play."

"I'm fourteen," I tell her. Sometimes I think she forgets.

"So? C'mon. Out. Go on." She points at the door. "Get out from under my feet for an afternoon and give us peace."

She slaps my legs again.

"But, Mam. There's nothing tae dae round here."

"Yer fourteen," she reminds me. "Ye'll find something."

Before she skelps my legs for a fourth time, I curse under my breath and get up. Three steps takes me tae the door, and then I swim through the rainbow-coloured fly blinds and out on tae the decking. The air is damp and close and thick, and it smells mouldy thanks tae the River Clyde that runs along the back ae the site.

"I'll shout ye in for yer tea. Dinnae be bothering me in the meantime."

The door slams behind me and a minute later, there's the muffled sound ae continuing, frantic, pointless housework.

Huda-huda-huda. Huda-huda-huda. Huda-huda-huda.

The caravan site is a circle ae red-chip stones that runs round a big patch ae long grass. There's maybe fifty caravans parked around the perimeter ae the circle. It takes five minutes tae dae a circuit if yer not in too much ae a rush. Five minutes. That's all. There's a shop that's always shut and a block ae communal toilets that always reeks ae pish. The nearest swing-park is a mile away. The nearest village is a wee bitty further, up a big stinking hill. There's no kids my age except for my wee sister, and she's off with my big brother tae get some messages from town. Even if she was here, she'd not be interested in playing with me. My big brother just disnae play anymore.

I sit down on the decking and stare at the end ae my

beak, gently banging my heid against the wooden handrail. I'm not doing any more or any less than I was a few minutes ago, but at least back then I was indoors and comfy. Inside the caravan, the sweeping finally comes tae an end and there's a wee moment ae silence before my mam puts the wireless on and tunes it in tae one ae her rubbishy big band stations. Cursing her again, I get up and wander off.

The family that owns the caravan—folk I've never met— keep a wee plot ae land running down its side where they grow their own tatties or carrots or whatever. My big brother had tried tae tend tae it and turn the earth over when we first arrived, but my mam warned him that he might damage whatever was growing, and so he left it alone. For a wee change, he was the one cursing my mam. His guid intentions are still planted in the ground, the shovel sticks up like a pole that's missing its scarecrow. I have a wee glance round. There's not another soul about. There really is nothing else tae dae.

I grab the shovel out from the ground and head up a wee embankment tae a copse ae conifers that separate the caravan part from the river. Under the cover ae the branches, the ground never really gets enough sun tae dry out so it's always damp and soft and when I stab the blade ae the shovel intae the dirt, it glides in like it's slicing through a chocolate fudge cake and when I scoop it out, the muck holds in one wobbly, muddy piece, balanced on the end ae the blade. Twisting the handle in my hand, the shovel empties with a wet shloomp.

"This is it," I say tae myself. "This is what I'm doing with my holidays."

I dig the shovel in again and lift out another chunk ae earth. Shloomp. It falls on top ae the first load and now there's a hole in the ground that I can squeeze my foot intae. It's big enough tae take my whole shoe. The sole'll be mawkit now, I decide. My mam'll go fucking radge if I trail this through the caravan. But I'm outside. I'm doing what I'm told. And if I keep at it, I'll end up building up my muscles like my big brother. I take a third shovel-load. And a fourth. And a fifth, and now I can fit both feet in the hole if I scrunch them up. When I step out, both shoes are caked in mud, looking like I've stepped in a massive dug shite. I have to laugh. My mam's going to go through the fucking roof, so she will.

13

The hole is coming on grand, and I end up sorta enjoying myself, but it's hot work, and after a wee bit, I need tae take my jumper off. Even though I'm just in my t-shirt and jeans now, the sweat still dribbles down my back. At this rate, I reckon it'll not be long before I'm stripped tae the waist, which would seem pretty daft given that it's not long stopped raining, it's dead close, and it looks like it'll not be long before it's pishing it down again. The palms ae my hands—especially round about where my thumb and forefinger meet—throb yon heavy, thick way that I ken means I'll barely be able tae hold on tae a knife and fork tomorrow. My big brother would tell me that's because I'm not used tae manual labour, I dinnae dae fuck all when I'm helping round the house, and I'm always skiving off. He says all this like he thinks it's a bad thing.

There's nae skiving off today, though. I've got a hole tae dig. It's about a yard in length and width, and it's deep enough now that I need tae plant myself inside it so I can reach down without breaking my back. The changes in the earth, even in just the bit I've done so far, are mental. There's clay, stone, and mud in the cross-sections I'm looking at. It even looks like there's a bit ae sand in there. Through it all, roots hang out like bits ae string and rope. Everything's holding together well, though, and the sides are firm.

With the amount ae rain we'd had on this holiday, the river is fat and fast-flowing and it rumbles as it races on tae Glasgow. It's so loud, I probably couldnae hear my mam supposing she was shouting on me from the caravan door and—thank fuck—I cannae hear her with her carpet sweeper. But I hear myself panting as I'm digging and I hear the sludgy noise as I lift the dirt out and I definitely hear the almighty crack when the shovel cuts intae the earth as I take another load.

The crack sounds deep and wooden, and I think I've maybe hit a thicker root from one ae the bigger trees but then my mind jumps tae creepy-crawlies. In the heap ae dirt I've excavated so far, there's more beasties than I would've expected, so there is, and it's not just worms. There's sick-looking spiders with big, see-through bodies and spindly wee legs. There's been a centipede and a millipede that both gave me the heebie-jeebies and made me realise that the more legs a beastie's got, the more shitty-feart ae it I'm likely tae be. There's even been a coupla things I didnae even ken what tae call; wee alien creatures with weird, swollen bodies that didnae like the light and burrowed their ugly frames intae the muck like their lives depended on it.

I'm fourteen now, I remind myself. I'm a big, brave laddie so I don't run away or anything, but yon big crack gives me the feeling like my jaw's trying tae disappear down my throat, and I jump the hell out ae the hole, leaving the shovel planted in the dirt.

I'm not even out for ten seconds before it starts tae happen.

Around the blade of the shovel, beetles start leaking out ae the ground, pouring out, streaming out. Black, shiny beetles and they look like oil, like blood seeping out ae a wound. I dinnae ken if there's such a thing as a beetle's nest, but if there is, I reckon I've hit one.

There's hundreds ae the wee fuckers, all scuttling about, running along the top ae each other, clawing their way up the sides ae the hole, clawing up the shovel and then falling back down on tae their backs, and now the bottom ae the hole is alive, swimming with them and the way their legs clatter and click, it sounds like they're talking tae each other.

"Oo-ya bastard," I mutter. I'm brushing myself down, suddenly itchy, so I am, and my t-shirt that had been clean on this morning gets covered in mud and dirt.

And now it gets a wee bitty worse because now the shovel trembles in the ground. It's not a lot, but it's there. The force and pressure ae the beetles is making it vibrate. I take a step back. Then another step. And with the third step, the bottom ae the hole disappears out ae sight. Although I cannae see them, they're louder than ever, and I even start tae think I can smell them.

There's a rumble ae thunder in the distance. The river moves even faster now, startled like a horse with a skelped arse.

Another crack. Lighter. Nowhere near as bassy. Behind me. Instinct grabs my heid and spins me around.

The lassie looks about my age, maybe a bitty younger, dead pretty with dark hair and a wee splattering ae freckles across her nose and she's standing there in a green, long-sleeved t-shirt and blue jeans. Her foot is planted on what must be the only twig in the whole copse that's dry enough tae snap.

"Whit ye doing?" she asks. Her voice is light. Not just light as in the opposite ae heavy, but light as in the opposite ae dark, too. It's a warm voice, and I smile at her for a second until I remember I'm fourteen, mucky, standing out on my own at a dirty big hole, and I was about tae run away from a few hundred beetles, and next I ken, I'm brushing myself down again, making myself dirtier.

"Nothing," I say with a frown. "How? What are you doing, likes?"

She shrugs and looks round about her. "I'm not doing anything." Then she steps off the twig and walks like she's heading over tae the hole. "What ye digging?"

I panic. I dinnae ken why. I step in front ae her, blocking her way, my cheeks burning up intae the mother ae all beamers.

"I'm not digging nothing. I'm not doing nothing. That was there when I got here."

She stops walking and starts tae laugh.

"Aye, right, then. I seen ye," she insists. She howks a thumb over her shoulder. "I was just over there. Two seconds ago, ye were standing in that hole with that spade in yer hand, digging. I seen ye. I stood and watched ye."

"No, I wasnae. No, ye didnae. And it's a shovel, not a spade."

"What's the difference?"

I pause. "I dinnae ken."

"Well, then. Stop being a choob and tell me what yer doing."

She puts a hand on my arm and pushes past me. I mean tae try and stop her again, but that touch just slows everything down and for a wee moment, the river freezes, the sky's like a black and white photo and I dinnae care what she thinks about me because, for a minute, it disnae matter. Like I'm moving through a clear pea soup, I turn tae watch her walk over tae the hole and I want tae warn her about the beetles and the see-through spiders and all the other beasties, but the words dinnae come, and by the time I get something that makes sense worked out, she's already there. She stands with her hand on her hips and peers down, shaking her heid. Now I feel even more ae a fanny for backing off, but then my eyes practically burst out of their sockets when without as much as a word ae warning, she jumps intae the fucking hole, so she does.

"It isnae very deep," she says, all matter ae fact. "What ye burying? A budgie?"

"My legs come back tae me, and I storm across tae her, not giving a fuck about them beetles anymore. "I told ye," I say, "I'm not doing nothing. I'm not digging nothing. I'm not burying nothing. I'm..."

And at that, I can see that the beetles are gone. They've vanished. They've crawled back down intae their nest or wherever it is they live and all that sits at the bottom ae the hole is a wee puddle ae dirty water that's gathered around the shovel. The lassie looks up at me looking down, and she starts tae scan the ground, trying tae see what I can see, unaware that what I can see isnae there tae be seen. She looks back up at me, confused.

"Lose something?" she asks.

It disnae take long. It takes about as long as it takes for me tae realise that something's not right, like that feeling ye get when ye think ye've been somewhere before, but ye ken ye havnae. My knee buckles. I very nearly keel over. It's all too much. It's like all the air has been sucked out ae me and those two words are dense, and they buzz around my brain, choking it, and they sting. I feel punched and hurt, but then I decide that maybe these words have been stolen from me. It feels like the words were something I should've said and I wonder where the sun's got to, why the sun keeps disappearing.

"Eh?" I manage, but not immediately. Some time has passed, I'm aware. It takes a while. Everything is taking a while.

"Did ye drop yer sweetie when ye were digging yer hole for yer wee budgie?"

"Eh?"

"Are. You. All. Right?" she asks.

"Eh?" I say again, and then the penny drops, the air comes back, and the sun reappears. "Aye. Aye, I'm fine. And I told ye, there isnae a budgie."

She reaches out to me. "Gimme a hand, then."

At first, I'm not sure about that, given what happened the last time she touched me, plus my fingernails are black with muck, but she's looking like she's running out ae patience with me and even though she's coming across quite snippy, her voice is still warm and light and I sense I probably want tae keep it that way. I take her hand—a wee bitty disappointed when there's no buzz this time— and I lean back and pull her out. It disnae take much effort. She's not very heavy.

"Sorry," I say. "My hand's all mawkit, so it is."

"It'll wash off."

And then, again without warning, she turns, reaches

across the hole and grabs the handle ae the shovel and I can see what she's about tae dae by the shape ae her arm, and I get a bad feeling so I take a breath tae tell her tae hold on a wee minute but the whole thing's happening too quickly, and I dinnae have the time. The ground is so soft she disnae need tae pull hard, and the shovel slips out ae the earth with a watery smack.

Maybe I thought the shovel was a plug. Maybe I expected the hole tae fill tae the brim with beetles gushing out ae the ground. But nothing comes out. Nothing happens. Nothing except when the lassie plucked the shovel from the hole she sent something flying intae the air and now that it's starting tae drift back down tae earth, I can see what it is. It's a long, dirty-white feather.

12

The numbers, as he passed them, began to crumble and decay and he found his attention drifted to their deconstruction because it happened so silently and so elegantly and without a breath of fuss. As it went on, it became harder to keep an eye on the numbers he still had to pass by on his way to zero because he knew their fate and he couldn't warn them, but he knew the importance of keeping count. He knew he had come so far. He didn't want to start again. He didn't know if starting again was allowed.

<h1 style="text-align:center">11</h1>

t hangs in the air right in the middle ae me and the lassie, bang in line between our eyes. It hardly moves except the individual wee barbs twitch in the softest ae breezes. It cannae be like that, though. There must be a thread holding it up. There must be some prick up a tree with a fishing road trying tae make us look like a pair ae fannies.

"Are ye sure yer feeling alright?" she asks.

"Dae ye not think that's amazing?"

"Aye. Ye can go cock-eyed. Big wows."

"Eh?"

My focus loosens from the feather and ontae the lassie. She's staring right back at me. Her right eyebrow's lifted, and her mouth's pinched in. I nearly laugh because she actually does look genuinely concerned for me, despite the fact she hasnae a clue who I am, and everything she kens about me hardly shows me off at my finest.

"Are ye blind?" I ask, smiling. "Can ye not see that?"

"See what?"

Slowly, because I dinnae want tae disturb it, I reach out, my finger and thumb poised in a claw, ready tae pluck the feather out ae the air. Before I can get too close tae it, her own hand shoots out and skelps mine away.

"Hoy! What's your game?" she demands, suddenly not looking quite as understanding as she was a couple ae seconds ago.

"Ow! I'm showing ye the feather."

"The feather?"

"Aye."

"A bird's feather?"

"No, a dug's feather. Of course a bird's feather."

"From yer budgie?"

It's too late. It's gone.

"Are ye sure ye didnae see it?" My gaze drops tae the ground, assuming that we must've wafted it down with all our chattering. There's no sign ae it.

"I'm positive."

"When ye ripped the shovel out the hole, ye pinged a feather intae the air. Are ye sure yer sure?"

She's still holding on tae the shovel, but her grip is loose and there's no resistance when I yank it from her grasp. Now I've got it back I dinnae ken what tae dae with it, so I end up spearing it back intae the hole, only worried about what I might disturb after it's stuck in the ground.

"I'm becoming sure ae a few things today, aye," she says, "but yer feather's not one ae them."

Over her shoulder, maybe twenty yards away, there's a wee twinkle. Something catches one ae the few shafts ae light that've been determined enough tae break through the heavy sky and leaves and branches, and all that shite and the feather's caught and lit as it hovers a few feet above the worn path that snakes through the copse.

"There," I say, all excited, pointing tae the shimmer behind her.

She turns tae follow my finger and the way she leans slightly tae the left and right like she's trying different angles, tells me she still disnae see it.

I curse tae myself and barge by her, heading off towards the twinkle. "Here," I say, but I've already lost sight ae it.

"Hey dinnae get angry with me," she says. "It's not my fault yer mental."

"It was over here."

I'm beyond the point ae the twinkle now and there' still

no sign ae it either on the breeze or on the ground. Its disappearance forces me down one ae two roads. I can either let it go and be content that a complete stranger thinks I'm a total windae-licker, or I can march on, determined tae find the feather. The first option, while it'd probably be easier in the long run, leaves me with the problem that the only think I've got tae keep myself occupied for the rest ae the afternoon is digging that fucking hole, and that's lost some ae its appeal now I've got an audience. There's really only one choice here, so there is, and that's tae follow the feather tae the ends ae the earth until I find it, or until the lassie gets bored with me and fucks off tae dae something else, something less stupid. Of course, there's an other option; an option fit for a fourteen-year-old laddie and an approximately similarly aged lassie but I'm so mawkit I cannae even let the idea warm its feet before scurrying it out.

"Where ye going?" she asks.

"I told ye," I say as I storm off. "There was a feather."

"Em, newsflash. We're outside. There's birds everwhere. Birds have feathers. Ken?"

"It was a dirty-white feather."

"So it came from a dirty-white bird. Where's the mystery?"

"The mystery is why I've got tae explain myself over and over. It came out ae the ground. It came out ae the hole. It was hovering in front ae us for ages."

And that's it, I decide. I've explained it as best I can. I'm not going through it all again. If she disnae understand it, fine. So be it. So I march on, my beak pointed at the path, and it must look like I think I'm sniffer dug trying tae pick up the scent. That's only partly true. Mostly, I'm watching my step because while this is a path ae sorts, there's still plenty tae trip me up. The ground's uneven and tough, thick ropes ae roots spurt out ae the earth, squiggle along for a bit before diving back under, making perfect hoop traps for an unsuspecting foot. The further we go on, the thicker the trees become, and the more likely they are tae be on the actual path.

Just as I'm starting tae think the lassie's given up and I start tae feel like a useless choob for not at least trying tae chat her up, she decides tae pipe up, and at the same time, the feeling goes away.

"In case yer worried that ye might've missed it," she says, "I've not seen anything back here neither."

I dinnae say anything and speed up a notch, using my arms now tae swing round the tree trunks as the path continues tae weave and wind.

"Have ye been down this way before?" she asks.

I dinnae rise tae it and even when a rabbit dashes across my path, I manage tae keep a wee startled squeak swallowed down, so I dae.

"Dae ye even ken where yer going?"

I roll my eyes at this and allow myself a sleekit wee grin. It's a path. There's only two ways ye can go; forward and backward. It disnae get any more complicated than that. Right enough, though, the trees are getting much thicker now, and the path's getting much thinner and more difficult tae make out, and for the first time, I actually have tae climb over the gap between two trunks because they're too close together tae walk through. At this point, I try tae remember exactly when it was that I stopped looking for the feather.

And now there's bushes tae the side ae me; thick bushes with thorns like razors sticking out ae them and they're so close tae what's left ae the path that I'm snagging my jeans on them with practically every step I'm taking.

"Watch yer step through here," I say.

"You worry about yerself," she fires back. "I'm not the one that disnae ken where we're going."

Although she's had this cock-sure attitude since we met, it's probably the first time that I twig that she might be a stranger tae me, but she's not a stranger tae this place. She's been through this copse before, and as much as I hate tae admit it, I've not. I really dinnae ken where we're going.

Whatever. I plough on, slower than ever with the bushes and trees and what not, and it's getting awfy dark this deep intae the copse and it now the ground is littered with the wee caps ae different fungus and there, two foot ahead ae me, there's a mushroom the size ae a dinner plate hanging from the bark ae a tree, looking like it belongs in a fairy tale. I glance over my shoulder tae see if she's still at the back ae me, this time more for reassurance than anything else.

"Found it yet?" she asks when she see's me looking.

I face forwards again. Even in this twilight, she's awfy pretty. Much prettier than any ae the dugs at my school. I smile and feel myself blush. "Not yet."

"Ye still looking?"

"Aye."

"Well, if ye dinnae find it in the next week minute, yer not gonnae find it. Of course, that's assuming there's something tae find in the first place."

Now I'm having tae push branches out the way before I can keep going, and even then I cannae avoid a few ae them scratching across my chest and neck until it gets tae the point I'm walking blind most of the time.

Then, just as I get the feeling we're about tae make it through and break intae thinning undergrowth and maybe even a bit ae a clearing, her hands land on my shoulders and she's either trying tae push me tae the ground, or she's trying tae jump on my back.

"What—"

"Get down," she growls, and she pushes harder, forcing me down on tae my hunkers.

I'm on all fours, my hands planted in something soft and damp that I hope is just muck. I look up and behind, and she looms over me, and at that moment I have no doubt that she could kill me right now if she wanted tae.

"What ye doing?"

"Wheesht," she hisses.

She's crouching as low down as she can get and she takes a coupla long, wide strides past me. She stops where the wee trail comes tae an end as it runs intae one ac them razor bushes. Without turning back tae me, she beckons me over. I take a look, and then a sniff, at my mucky hands, wipe them across the arse ae my jeans and then shuffle forward tae join her.

When I get tae her side, it takes a wee minute for my eyes tae land on whit she's wanting me tae see. First things first, there is indeed a clearing and compared tae the shadowy conditions here in the copse, it looks bathed in brilliant tropical sunlight, just a few feet ahead. Second, the clearing is a sandy peninsula where a wee stream—hardly any more than a truckle, so it isnae—winds its way intae the full swollen mass ae the Clyde.

It's when my eyes focus on the very tip ae the peninsula that I finally see what we're hiding from. There's a skinny man with grey hair casting a fishing line intae the Clyde before very slowly and deliberately reeling it back in. Once the line's back, he casts again, and the rod bends as it sways between the two and ten o'clock positions, and then it glides down tae the water, scribbling out a loopy signature ontae the surface.

It's hard tae judge just from the back ae the guy's heid, but he's maybe in his forties or fifties and dressed awfy smart in trousers and a blue shirt, looking more like's he's ready for a job interview or an appearance in court than a session out on the water.

"Who's that?" I whisper.

She disnae say anything.

"Is that yer father?" I try.

This time she reacts and shakes her heid, no. Meanwhile, the auld guy has turned tae get something out ae a wee wooden box he's got at his feet, and when I see his face, he looks much aulder. His eyes are dark and baggy, and skin on his face hugs the bone. He's not the happiest chappy I've ever clapped my eyes on, so he isnae.

"Had a sore paper round, that yin," I say.

She disnae react. Just keeps watching.

I get fed up. "Well, if he's not yer father, what are we hiding for?"

Her lips part as though she about tae say something, but then they close again, and she sighs out through her nose. Eventually, she turns tae me, and she's awfy serious.

She whispers, "We're not hiding. He kens we're here."

Ah let this sink in and try tae make sense ae it, but I've not got enough information. In terms ae maths at school, there's too many unknowns. That's what the teacher would say: too many unknowns, too many variables. I'm shite at maths, so I am, but I remember that much.

"Is that why yer digging yer hole?" she asks, still in a whisper. "Are ye setting a trap for that miserable auld bugger?"

"Eh? No. I'm just—" Then I remember. "And I amnae digging a hole. I told ye, that was there when I got there."

She nods and manages a smile like she's heard it all before, which of course she has. She starts tae back away, and next I ken, she's leading the way back along the path. I'm following her.

10

My hands look like elephant hide with all the dried dirt. When I pick it off, it comes away in chunks and my skin's wet underneath and a deep pink. My t-shirt is like some crappy camouflaged tie-dye affair; the bulk ae it's still white, but there are swirls ae muck and sweat and grass. I dinnae even want tae look at my jeans. There's patches ae mud at the knees that might brush off, but I cannae see how I'm going tae avoid a tanning from my mam when I get back tae the caravan.

Surprisingly, the lassie looks as clean and tidy as she did when I first seen her. There's not so much as a hair out ae place. Her clothes might as well have just come off the washing line. Her green t-shirt still has a freshly ironed look about it. Lassies, I think tae myself. It's just not fair.

Another thing that isnae fair is that she's far more graceful than me as she winds herself round tree trunks and through bushes and branches. She has nature on her side, I suppose, and because I'm behind her, I get a better chance tae give her a wee deck all over. She's a very compact wee thing, I decide. Guid wee arse on her. Nice arms. Meanwhile, I'm still a clattering hulk behind her. Christ alone kens what she must've been thinking about me on the outward trip. Then again, she didnae disappear. She kept following me all the way. She didnae have tae, so she didnae.

"It's funny, eh?" I say.

"What is?" She disnae break stride let alone look back.

"It always takes longer tae get somewhere than it does tae get back."

"That's yer funny observation, aye?"

"Aye, well it's true. I remember when I was a wee laddie and my big brother was taking me intae town tae get my birthday present. It would take ages. The bus would be the slowest in the country. It would take longer tae drop folk off and pick folk up. Then after we'd got the present, the bus home would be like a fucking train, so it would. Whoosh! It would zoom home like it was our own private bus."

The path widens now, and I'm able tae jog on a wee bit, so we're more like side by side.

"That's yer experience?"

I nod, struggling tae remember what my point was that I as trying tae make. "Aye. More or less."

"See, in my experience, it's the other way around. My anticipation would be higher on the way home. It would be the bus home that would be slowest for me."

"No way. Aye?"

"Aye."

"That's mental."

She goes on, "And what that tells me about you, is that for you, the possession is a bigger deal than the application." She suddenly sounds much aulder than me, much cleverer.

"Eh?"

"Buying the toy car is more important tae ye than playing with the toy car."

I have tae think about it, but it's not easy because I was never really that in tae toy cars.

"No, I did enjoy playing. Of course I did."

"I'm not saying ye didnae."

"Then what are ye saying?"

"I'm saying that the bigger deal for you is having the car in its box, in yer wee handie."

"Maybe. Acht, I dinnae ken. But yer making it out like I'm being a fanny about it."

"I'm not saying it's wrong either. It's just different, that's all. In fact, given the situation we're in, and the way things are, that might be the most sensible place tae be."

I'm not really understanding her again, and then I remember something that probably isnae relevant, but before I can decide properly, I'm already talking. "It's like when I was going tae my auntie's for my dinner. I hated going tae my auntie's. Everybody hates going tae their aunties, I suppose. Anyway, getting there would take ages. Absolutely ages. Coming back..." I snap my fingers. "Like that. Blink ae an eye."

She thinks for a moment, her gaze interested at the branches above us.

"That's the exact same thing," she says. "Except yer swapping anticipation with dread."

"Well, what about the time when I'm going—"

"Aw, for fuck's sake," she says and then she stops dead in her tracks, grabs ma heid, plants her lips on mine and instantly, my heart starts zinging about inside me like a bouncy ball and because her hands are on my ears, I can hear my pulse thunder inside me, as loud as a peel ae thunder, so loud I can feel it in my toes, and her touch is firm but her lips are soft and wet and she opens her mouth a wee bitty and clamps my bottom lip between hers and then she does the same with my top lip but there's never a point that her face isnae touching mine and she goes between the top and bottom lip a couple ae times and then she pushes her tongue intae ma mouth and the tip ae it caresses ma tongue and she tastes ae spearmint chewing gum and I didnae realise I had my eyes shut until I open them tae see she's got hers closed lightly and I notice that her eyebrows are the most beautiful things I've ever seen, so beautiful that I have tae shut my eyes again in case I'm imagining them, and then I go tae take a hold of her heid in my hands but I'm scared that I won't be able to feel her, that this is stupid dream, that she's not real, so my hands just hang there in mid air, somewhere near her ears and now her tongue is running along the edges ae my lips, the softest thing I've ever felt in my life, the most perfect temperature ae anything I've ever felt in my life, the most I've ever felt like I was home, and with my eyes shut, all I can see is pink but the shade drifts deeper from left tae right, doing this three times, making me think we've been standing here for days like this, or spinning in circles and when it stops, when she pulls away, my eyes are still shut, my mouth is still parted open, my arms are still up and my hands are still not quite touching her face and right at that second, I feel like I ken exactly what she means when she's talking about anticipation because already I miss the way that made me feel.

"There," she says. "Now shut the fuck up."

9

The further he got into his count, the quicker the numbers seemed to pass him by. He couldn't imagine how fast they'd pass once he approached the end, but the idea excited him, thrilled him, almost as much as it terrified him and filled him with dread. He suspected that when these sensations were all boiled down, they were the exact same thing.

8

f I think this is gonnae be the start ae some smoldering holiday romance, I've got another thing coming. It really does look like she just wanted me tae shut the fuck up because when I open my eyes properly, she's already scooting off along the path, and the prospect ae another spot ae winching disnae seem that likely. I cannae even begin tae consider how disappointed that makes me feel.

In the near distance now, just about the same distance away again, I spot the handle ae the shovel sticking out ae the hole. She walks towards it, she looks at it, walks by and in time with all this, my heart rises and sinks.

"Where ye going?" I ask, practically shouting.

"Away."

Although she's walking quickly, I can run much faster, and I catch up easily.

"Away? Why?"

"I shouldnae have done that," she says.

Now I'm in line with her, I can see she's all red and flushed like maybe she's been crying.

"It's alright," I say, going for light-hearted. "Ye wanted tae shut me up. Ye shut me up. Maybe it didnae last long, but for a while, it did the job. Ye can shut me up again if ye like."

I step in front of her, and we stop. I give her what I hope is a warm, friendly, no problem sorta smile. She disnae smile back.

"Ye dinnae understand," she says.

"It wasnae that bad, was it?"

"Ye really dinnae understand."

I laugh. It's the result ae that popular combination ae nerves and putting a brave face on things. There's no humour in there because although she's right and maybe I dinnae understand, I think I understand enough.

"What is there tae understand? It's a bit ae banter, so it is. I mean, it's not as if there's anything else tae dae around here."

Despite the fact I seriously doubt that this is the password tae make everything all shining bright again, she finally smiles back at me. It disnae last, though, and then she drops her heid and walks by me.

"I'll see ye around," she says.

I want tae go after her, but I ken it won't change anything. In fact, it'll somehow make things worse. The bee has taken up residence in the bonnet. So I stand next tae the hole and watch her walk away, let her walk away, not in a hurry, looking kinda weary, heading for whatever caravan round the circle is hers. Then something so basic strikes me, I actually slap myself on the foreheid.

"I dinnae ken yer name," I shout.

She keeps on walking and raises an arm either tae wave cheerio, or tae let me ken she hears me, but I'm left with nothing other than the thought of what a fucking mental day it's been so far.

I stand about for a while, kicking up dirt, wondering what tae dae, wondering if maybe I should've gone after her, wondering what I did that was so wrong, wondering how I could've been so stupid as not to ask her name, wondering why she never thought tae ask me mine, wondering why I can never come up with the right thing tae say, wondering what time it is. All this does is make me more frustrated with how things ended up, and eventually this frustration turns intae pure anger. None ae my wonderings have provided any answers, so I cannae even put my finger on what exactly I'm angry at, other than everything's just a big fat bag ae fucking shite, and the only thing worse than feeling this angry is having no one tae take it out on. Then I spy the shovel.

I jump down the hole and grab the shovel and then I'm stabbing at the ground, breaking it up, not really digging, not really caring if the beetles come back because even if they dae, I'll fucking show they wee cunts who's the boss and I'll chop them intae dust. That's what I tell myself.

The longer this goes on, the more the motion feels like I'm really paddling along in a canoe and without trying, I deVELop a BEAT

as I'm STABBing the GROUND
and the MUCK and the SHITE
is REAlly ma MAM
and her STUpid iDEA
for COMING out HERE
tae be BORED out my TITS
aWAY from my PALS
with NOTHing tae DAE
and the DAYS just rePEAT
and MERGE intae ONE
and SO it goes ON
til I'm LOSing ma BREATH
and my ARMS feel like LEAD
and my FACE burns bright RED
and my HEID starts tae SPIN
and my CHEST's fit tae BURST
and I WANT tae sit DOWN
'cause the AIR's still too CLOSE
but I'm LOST in the BEAT
and I NEED tae keep GOING
til the SWEAT starts tae POUR
from the END ae my BEAK
and it DRIPS on the GROUND
but it DISnae look RIGHT
'cause It's FLOating on TOP
ae a SPLAtter ae BLOOD
and I HUVnae a CLUE

if it's COMing from ME, so I stop and chuck the shovel tae one side.

I fall back, my arse plunking down on the edge ae the hole. I pant, sucking huge lungfuls ae oxygen, trying tae get it round my body and uptae my brain so the colour will come back tae my vision. I waft the bottom ae my t-shirt that's so wet it feels like soggy tissue paper, but it's enough to encourage some sticky air tae wrap round my skin, and I start tae cool down. I dab my nose, my heid, check my hands—front and back—dab my nose again, spit on the ground. The blood isn't mine.

Still sitting, I bend over for a closer look. My heid drops between my knees, and I stare at the red dribble that's oozing out ae the ground. It's not a lot. It's maybe half a cup at the very most. My first thought is that I've stabbed through that beetle nest, but as satisfying as that thought is, there's actually too much blood for that. To be honest, I dinnae even ken if beetles have blood.

I reach down and wipe the tip ae my index finger across the damp ground. The blood is a deep, rich colour but water thin. It reminds me so much ae red wine, my finger rises tae my mouth, offering the stain tae my tongue and it's only last second alarms ae disgust that stop me. A year ago, I tell myself, when I was less awkward than I am now, I'd've tasted it anyway. I'm still tempted when I spot another colour down there in the wee canal left by my trailing finger.

It's a tiny patch ae white.

It disappears back under the red, so I stick my finger back in, deeper this time, and I drag the blood away. I see the white again. Maybe it's a bone. Whatever it is, it warms my finger. Another few fingers join in the dig, pushing away dirt and blood, creating a hole within a hole. Whatever the white is, it's turned pink and it isnae bone. It's too soft to be bone. And maybe I kent all along that it wasnae bone. Maybe now I realise—or admit—that it's a feather.

I cannae think. If I think, I'll stop, and there's something about this and the wee twinkly I saw on the path that tells me I need tae carry on, I need tae get this done quickly before I change my mind. This is important. More fingers join in, then fingers become hands, and the hands are shovels, digging, scratching and pushing muck out the way. The longer it takes, the quicker I move, becoming desperate for it to be over because, despite this determination, the sensation ae dirt and shite gathering under my fingernails starts tae freak me out. It's not such a big jump from scratching my way down and in tae scratching my way up and out.

As quick as I'm moving, it still takes a while. The thing I'm uncovering isnae wee. It has mass. It has shape and curves. And maybe I can't see it properly because I'm far too close tae it.

Eventually, I work my way round the shape and get tae the top left corner ae the bottom ae the hole, near where I began. The shape tapers intae something long and narrow and harder than the rest, more brittle. And then, I'm done. It's over.

It's over.

I'm exhausted and so filthy that it must look like somebody's dug me up, but it's done. I hop out ae the hole, wiping the stream ae sweat off my brow with the back ae my hand. It's a bit late now tae be worried about the kicking I'm gonnae get from my mam when she sees me and when I look down and see what I've uncovered, none ae it matters anyway. I wipe away more sweat, this time out ae my eyes.

It's lying out, looking like one ae they side-on pictures ye see in them Egyptian tombs, like a hieroglyphic something. It's not fully dug out or uncovered, but I can still tell what it is. I dinnae need tae see its legs or the back end ae its body. I can fill in the blanks. The body, neck, heid, and beak are enough for me to see it's a stork and the second—the very instant—I think that word, it opens its eye, lifts its heid off the ground and stares right at me.

7

The stork seems tae be staring slightly off-stage, over by the river, but it's only the heid that's pointing that way. Its eye is firmly on me.

I meet its gaze. It's impossible to look anywhere else. Its eye is so big and human, with a wide pupil and an iris that's brown like a milky coffee. It never seems to blink. Its heid's still raised off the ground, so I ken it's alive, but even if its whole body was laid out and its tongue was hanging out, it still widnae look deid. That eye isnae lifeless. That's the key. It might not be blinking. It might not be moving, and there's a small pink wound on its side where I guess I caught it with the shovel, but ye can tell it's alive just by looking in that one eye. And like I ken it's alive, I ken it's eyeing me up, sussing me out, maybe wondering if I'm about tae jump it.

It neednae worry. My legs dinnae work right now. My thighs and calves are like stone. My knees and ankles are dry and seized up. I'm absolutely no danger to it. The only bit ae me working is my brain, ticking away double time tae assess all ae this. Considering my reaction tae a few beetles, I'm coping better, but maybe it's shock rather than a steel nerve that's responsible.

I mean, it's a just bird. And aye, okay, so it's a bird that up tae a few minutes ago was buried alive in the middle ae a copse, in the middle ae nowhere, and unless it was buried while me and that lassie were away spying on the fisherman, it might've been lying there alive for years somehow, but it's still just a bird. And as long as I'm able tae keep on telling myself that, I might not pass out.

It's just a bird whose body is starting tae expand. Beforehand, it'd been dead slender and smooth, but now the shape ae each feather becomes clearer and what was slim starts tae fill out like a ball, like it's inflating, and then when it looks like it might fucking explode, it's just a bird that gives itself an absolutely mental shoogle, sending feathers and dirt and mank flying in all roads, bits ae muck pinging off my chest and face.

It's just a bird that...well, I dinnae ken, it clears its throat or something. It coughs, it's beak open and pointed tae the sky like it's swallowing a fish, and then, with a burst ae flapping wings that kicks up even more dirt, it flips upright ontae its feet.

It's just a bird. It's just a bird.

It's just a bird, it's just a stork, that is a far scarier beast now standing up than it was when it was lying down. It's dirty beige feathers look like a fur coat. From my standing point, it looks about the same height as my mam—five feet—,but it's not until it stretches out its wings that I get a true sense ae its size. It is fucking massive, so it is. The tip ae one wing across to the tip of the other must be twice its height, and when them wings start tae flap in a wee test run, it's like leaning intae a fucking hurricane. My hair blows out from my face and the sweat chills on my brow. My t-shirt ripples. I find it hard tae catch a breath, hard tae keep my eyes on it. Eventually, I have tae turn away tae breathe and as I do I remind myself that this isnae all that strange. The poor thing's been buried for God knows how long. Makes sense that it'll want to give itself a wee stretch now that it's up and about, check to see everything's in working order. This is all perfectly normal.

It's just a bird that after the stretch and wee wing test, its body melts back intae its smooth, sleek stance. A lot ae muck has fallen off during the display, but it's still dead manky. It looks at me as if deep in thought and then, without warning, its beak plunges intae the mass ae dirty feathers and it growls as it preens itself.

My joints have loosened up now. The lead in my muscles has melted away. Just a bird? Is it fuck just a bird. With it distracted, I dinnae need a clearer invitation, and I fucking hammer it back tae the caravan.

It's not far, but it seems tae take forever and there's a whining noise in my ears that I eventually realise is me. When I burst out ae the copse and see the caravan, it gets worse, it gets so much more frantic and urgent and when I stumble down the embankment I can sense the stork at my back, its beak sharp as a blade, snipping and snapping at the arse of my jeans, tearing it to ribbons. And when I see the caravan door, it gets worse still, and my back starts tae burn as the pitch ae the whine increases, becomes more obviously my voice and then finally a single long, stretched out word:

"Mmmmmmmmmmmmmaaaaaaaaaaaaaam!"

Any last drops ae cool and calm vanish when I bound up the steps ae the deckin in twos and start banging on the door.

"Mam! Mam! It's me! Open up!"

I nearly said help. I came so close. So fucking close to shouting for help.

I batter the door again and then remember tae try the handle. My sweaty hand slips off it a couple of times, and when I get a decent grip and push it down, it doesn't budge. The door's locked.

I bang on the door again, practically punching it now.

"Mam! Open the door, Mam!"

It's impossible to stay in such a heightened state ae alert for too long. Eventually, ye start tae wonder why ye've not been picked down tae the bone, that maybe the threat isnae as urgent as ye perhaps thought.

I stop banging on the door and allow myself tae check over my shoulder. The stork's there, and it has moved since I ran from it, but it's still over by the embankment, its beak still buried in its feathers that look even more like a fur coat now it's in proper light.

The heel ae my hand is red raw from hammering on the

metal frame ae the door. If she was in, surely she would've heard me. Keeping going until I break my hand isnae going tae make much ae a difference. So I hold my breath, stick my ear up against the glass in the door and listen.

Huda-huda-huda. Huda-huda-huda. Huda-huda-huda.

"I'm not fucking believing this," I mutter. "Mam! It's me!"

I bang on the door a couple more times then listen again.

Huda-huda-huda. Huda-huda-huda. Huda-huda-huda.

"Mam, will ye open this fucking door ya stupid fucking cow!"

The door bursts open, pushing me back on the decking where I lose my footing, flee through the air and in the instant before I crash tae the ground, landing square on my arse bone, I think tae myself that I kent this was gonnae happen.

I land facing the stork. Surprised by my attempt at flight, it takes a wee break from cleaning itself and looks at me, a piece ae muck or shite hanging from its beak. It must get bored awfy quick because a few seconds later and it's back tae whatever itch needs the most scratching.

"Whit did you say?" Mam screams at me. She's a heid poking through the rainbow-coloured fly blinds.

I prop myself up ontae my elbow and wince from the fire that's burning up my spine.

"The door," I say, teeth clenched against the pain.

"Aye, the door. What about the bloody door?"

I really cannae be bothered going through this right now when there are more important matters tae deal with. "The stork." I nod in its direction.

"Stork."

"Aye."

The rest ae her body emerges through the fly blinds, and she stands out on the decking, her arms folded, her foot tapping.

"Doors and storks. Billy, what in God's name are ye talking about and would ye look at yer bloody clothes. What've ye been up tae, laddie?"

"Mam—"

"Aw, would ye look at they bloody clothes. I sent ye out as sharp as a button and now look at ye. D'ye think I've got nothing better tae dae then run after the back ae ye? D'ye think I want tae be spending my holidays washing more clothes, clothes that I hung out tae dry yesterday? Ken, for someone as keen as you are tae remind folk that yer fourteen, ye spend most ae yer bloody time acting like yer four."

"But can ye no see the stork, Mam?"

There's a long pause, then she says, "Billy, I swear tae the Almighty if ye've been in at yer big brother's whisky—"

"What? No!"

"Or is it drugs? Hm? 'Cause I'll warn ye right now, young man, I can smell that whacky tabacky from a mile away."

Despite the pain, I roll my eyes. "Mam—"

"Then what's all this bloody stork business in aid ae?"

As I look back at the stork, it's in the middle ae giving itself another guid shoogle. More clumps ae muck ping out like mortars. I point at it, jabbing my finger at it.

"What's over there, Mam? What dae ye see over there?"

She scrunches up her eyes and peers across at the embankment. Whatever she sees—and she must see something—it's nothing out ae the ordinary. If she saw a massive big fuck off stork, I'd think she'd react with more than a stifled yawn. Massive big fuck off storks. That's so last year.

"Billy, son. I've got nae bloody idea what yer talking about, but I'll tell ye this. Ye dinnae get storks in Scotland. Gulls, aye. Sparrows, aye. Starlings, aye. Maybe even the occasional chaffinch. Storks...eh, no."

Gingerly, I push myself up tae my feet and hobble as quickly as I can back up the decking steps, prepared tae let it go.

"Fine," I concede. "There's nae stork."

"Excuse me," she says, "but where dae ye think yer going?"

I point tae the caravan, realizing that I ken what she's about tae say, that realisation sapping energy from every part ae my body until I begin to collapse.

She unfolds and then refolds her arms. "If ye think yer getting in here in your state, young man, just as I've got the place looking spick and span..."

"But, but mam..."

"Billy, I told ye tae amuse yerself for an afternoon. Ye've been outside for about ten minutes, and I'm not having ye trawling all yer muck through my lovely clean caravan. I'm not having it, son. It's my holidays too, and I'm wanting tae put my feet up and listen tae my programmes, so you just wait out here til yer big brother gets back from the town..."

She's still blethering away and bumping her gums as she turns and steps back intae the caravan, pulling the door shut behind her, and I'm left standing on the decking, looking over the vegetable patch at a stork that takes another wee break from preening itself tae stare at me, like it reckons it's got some unfinished business with me.

There's a noise out here that's clear over my breathing and the stork's growling. It's coming from inside the caravan.

Huda-huda-huda. Huda-huda-huda. Huda-huda-huda.

6

He noticed a hum in the background somewhere. At first, he thought of it as a drone. He wasn't sure there was much of a difference between the two but the sound—while it never actually stopped—permanently sounded like it was about to run out of breath. Drones, he thought, wouldn't do that. Drones would just go on and on and would never falter. Drones would never waver. So he settled on thinking of it as a hum, and once he'd made up his mind, the hum sounded warmer, friendlier, as though it approved of his decision. That was when he realised the hum had always been there, even when he couldn't hear it, and it had always surrounded him.

5

decide that my mam must've been exaggerating when she said I'd only been out for ten minutes. It must've been a throw-away line. A figure ae speech, maybe. Because the alternative isnae worth contemplating, that the two hours or more that have passed since she first chucked me out has passed in ten minutes is impossible tae comprehend. And while I cannae quite articulate tae myself the consequences ae time passing so slowly, I ken it cannae be good. I'm still mulling it over seconds, minutes, days, whatever later when the door ae the caravan opens up again.

I'm expecting my mam tae come out, maybe with a wee cup ae tea and a choccy biccy for me, maybe tae tell me that I can go inside after all and that aye, she did see the stork, and she was just ripping the pish out ae me when she said she couldnae.

I ken that's a load ae shite, but. If she's coming out it's more likely she's coming out tae fucking chuck something at me. The fly blinds ripple, and it's on the tip ae my tongue tae tell her not tae bother, I'll bugger off, but then there's movement, and a figure pushes out and steps on tae the decking. But it's not my mam.

It's a man. And not only that, it's a man I'm sure I recognise. My heid's still fucked up by the stork, so I cannae place him immediately, but when he turns tae close the door and I can check out the back ae his heid, it falls intae place. He's the fishing guy from the peninsula.

Based on the lassie's reaction tae him, along with the fact that he's been in my caravan, I'm more instantly afraid from him than I was from the stork. I take wee steps away, backing down off from the decking.

"Hullo again," the man says, cheery. He's locking the door, still with his back tae me, locking my mam intae the caravan.

I dinnae say a word.

"Turned out not such a bad day after all," he goes on. "Pretty close, right enough, Pretty humid. A storm's in the post. Ye can be sure ae that."

Again, I keep my mouth shut.

He picks up a rod that had been leaning against the side ae the caravan, and he bends down tae pick up his wooden box. He still disnae look directly at me, but as he walks off, heading towards the peninsula, he says, "Ye can join me if ye like."

And off he goes, not in any kinda hurry. Just an auld guy with his fishing gear, out strolling tae the water. That leaves me and the stork who's still preening himself at the embankment and not for the first time since she left, I wish the lassie was still here. Absently, my hand goes up tae my face, my fingers brushing the outside ae my mouth as I try tae remember what it felt like.

So I follow the guy as he walks round the circle. He's heading the same way me and the lassie walked when we were chasing after the wee twinkling feather, but he's going the more sensible way; the way that disnae involve squeezing himself down a squiggly path through the copse.

We're not side by side or anything like it, really. I keep my distance. He doesn't look back, but I can tell he kens I'm following him like I dinnae need tae look behind me tae ken the stork isnae there. The auld guy keeps his pace. I do likewise.

We leave the circle after a wee while and join a very clear, very flat path that takes us between two caravans then up over a wee hump and then down towards the wee trickle stream. Tae the left, I can see the copse, and from here it's bit hazy, like a bank ae greenish fog running across the horizon. It looks sick.

When we reach the stream, we turn and head tae the Clyde and the sandy peninsula. Part ae me expected the lassie tae be waiting for us, but she's not here. I scan round tae the copse and the razor bush where we hid a wee while ago. From this end, the bush disnae look as thick as it did when I was right behind it. All things considered, it was a pretty shite place tae hide. She's not there either.

The auld guy sets himself up at the tip ae the peninsula, facing the Clyde that's still fat and swollen as it rolls noisily by. He takes a lure or a fly or something—I dinnae ken much about fishing—and fastens it on tae the end ae his line. After that, it's the usual two and ten o'clock business and then the line's cast.

"Ye dinnae need tae hang about back there," he shouts. "I'm like the fish. I'm not likely tae bite."

"What were ye doing in my caravan with my mam?" I ask.

"Getting ready," he says.

"For what?"

"This."

And then I dinnae ken what else tae say.

He fishes for a while—maybe five minutes, maybe longer—and he disnae look at me at any point. He's happy tae cast out, reel in, and not catch any fish. He keeps himself tae himself. Bored, I try tae skim some stones across the wee stream, but it really is pointless. The stream is nowhere near deep enough for skimmers. But I keep trying, and he keeps trying, and neither ae us has any luck, but that disnae seem tae be the point.

"It's nice spending time with ye like this," the auld guy says. "It's a pity yer wee pal couldnae join us."

"So ye could see us right enough?"

"Well, there's not that many folk here, so the folk that are kinda stand out, ken?"

"D'ye ever catch anything?" I ask, changing the subject because this one is a wee bitty too weird.

He lets this lie like he's thinking about it, and then he says, "Not really."

"My big brother says that true insanity is doing the same thing over and over and expecting different results."

He pauses again, longer this time. "Does yer brother really say that?"

"I dinnae ken," I admit. "I heard it somewhere. Maybe I read it."

By this point, I've wandered forwards, so I'm at the shore of the Clyde. I'm still a distance from the auld guy, but now rather than looking like we're not together, we probably look tae anyone watching that we are together, but we dinnae get on with each other.

"I dinnae expect different results, though. I expect the same thing tae happen over and over again."

Then he's back tae cast and reel. Meanwhile, I stumble upon some lovely flat pebbles and have a bit more luck skimming them in the Clyde. I get a sixer and watch, fascinated as it bounces across the river before dribbling out like an African bird planting itself down in some lake. And that's when I see it.

The stork's standing on the bank on the other side ae the river and it stares right at me, growls for a bit and then it buries its beak intae its feathers and continues preening. Credit where it's due, the preening is making a difference. Overall, it's still pretty manky, but it's cleaner in places, and the pink wound from the shovel is almost completely gone.

"Apart from anything else," the auld guy says, "I'm not even sure there's that many fish in here anyway."

I frown and smile at the same time, and it's a nervous kinda expression. It's the sort ae face that ye pull when ye want tae hide the fact that yer really shitting yer pants. He's not looking so he disnae pick up on it. The stork, though, is another matter.

"Aye? Do ye not get awfy hungry?" I ask.

"I dinnae eat them. I chuck them back," he says. Again,

there's a long pause and then one almighty yawn, and then he says, "For all I ken, it's probably the same fish."

"Maybe the stork's eating them."

The only way I can tell that I said this and didnae just tink it is that for a wee second—a blink-and-ye've-missed-it wee second—the auld guy looks at me with his dark, sunken eyes and then quickly tries tae disguise it by looking back at his line.

"Oh, aye," he says. "There's a stork out there, is there?"

"Can ye see it?" I ask, sounding all optimistic, not meaning tae.

"No, son. I cannae see it."

"My mam cannae see it neither, but it's there. It's right over there on the other side ae the river."

"Aye, son. I believe ye."

My mouth dries up, and when I stare across the river, expecting tae see the stork ripping more mank out ae itself, it's looking up too. It's like someone's scratched a needle across a record.

"Really? Ye believe me?" My voice trembles.

"Of course. It'll be cleaning itself up, I suppose."

"But...but if ye cannae see it—"

"I dinnae think I'm meant tae see it. I dinnae think anyone's meant tae see it. I dinnae make up the rules tae any ae this, ye ken."

"And it's my rules? Is that it?"

"Well, let's just say they're more yours than they are mine." The auld guy casts the line out. He disnae look like expanding on this and he carries on with his casting and reeling like the only thing we've been talking about is the weather. I've no clue what tae ask next because there's no answer I could hear that's gonnae make this easier tae understand. So that's it, I reckon. Stalemate. Discussion over.

I chuck my last skimmer—kinda pretending tae aim for the stork—and then start tae head back towards the easy path back tae the circle, wondering if my mam'll let me in now. She might, I decide. I'm not any muckier than I was the last time she seen me.

"Hey, Billy," the auld guy says.

I hear my name and stop deid.

"I really did love spending time with ye again," he says.

I start tae walk away, trying tae keep all cool like, while my heart fucking thrashes in my chest.

"I ken this must feel like the whole world's in on the joke except for you," he says, "and I'm sorry about that. Like I said, it's not my rules. But for what it's worth, I never blamed ye, Billy. I kent what yer really like. Yer a guid laddie. Yer a guid son and a guid brother. Ye tried yer best."

He keeps talking beyond this, and I hear his words—they sink in—but I'm running after that. Running across the peninsula, over the stones and pebbles that border the wee stream, up the bluff, back on tae the circle and I dinnae stop running until I get back tae the decking and the door ae the caravan because I can hear footsteps behind me and I'm not at all sure they're human.

All the way, I have the auld guy's words bouncing in my heid and what he said to me last before I broke intae a sprint, after he told me about the joke and about me being a guid laddie, and they're words I remember saying or hearing or I remember hearing myself say, but I dinnae ken where or how.

"There's no going back now," he said. "There's no going back."

4

Huda-huda-huda. Huda-huda-huda. Huda-huda-huda. I'm not believing this. Not again. "Mam!"

Huda-huda-huda.   Huda-huda-huda.   Huda-huda-huda.

"Mam! I've had enough. I'm wanting in."

Huda-huda-huda. Huda-huda-huda. Huda-huda-huda.

"You and that fucking carpet sweeper," I mutter, and I kick the door.

The stork flaps as it lands at its wee spot between the caravan and the embankment, near the wee vegetable patch that seems tae have more weeds scattered across it that I remember.

"Beat it, ya manky big fucker," I say tae it, leaning towards it like I'm hissing.

It reacts with as much nonchalance as a stork can possibly muster and bends its heid down so it can nibble on the feathers at the base ae its neck.

Without even realising I'm doing it, I'm still chapping on the caravan door, but I'm doing it in a half-hearted way. I'm not expecting to be chapping on my mam's heid any time soon.

Huda-huda-huda. Huda-huda-huda. Huda-huda-huda.

She's not gonnae let me in. She told me as much. And now I'm thinking that my big brother and my wee sister have been away for an afwy long time.

I take a seat on the decking—the same seat that I took all that time ago, and I start tae bang my heid against the handrail with a bit more force than earlier, and I find that I'm doing it in time with the rattle from the carpet sweeper.

"She's not gonnae let ye in."

The lassie in the green t-shirt is standing on the circle at the end of the caravan away from the river. I don't stop banging my heid even though I ken how it must look.

"Aye," I say. "I'd worked that out, so I had."

"Yer gonnae hurt yerself."

I dinnae say anything because I'm still pissed off with her.

"Seriously," she says. "Can ye knock it off? It's beginning tae freak me out."

"There's a stork standing over there," I say, still hitting my heid off the wooden handrail.

"Is there?"

I ken that she cannae see it, but she disnae react like she disnae believe me. She's expecting me tae say something like this. The joke really is on me. The auld guy was right.

"Aye. It's over there by the vegetable patch, near the embankment."

"Okay. What's it doing?"

I have tae stop banging my heid for a wee second so's I can check it out, but once I've had a look, I start banging again, still in time with the carpet sweeper.

Huda-huda-huda. Huda-huda-huda. Huda-huda-huda.

"It's cleaning itself. Surprise sur-fucking-prise."

"There's still time," she says, more tae herself, I think, than tae me.

"Time for what?"

I watch her. I see her scuffing her foot across the dirt, her hands planted deep in her jeans pockets, her arms perfectly straight. Her heid's dropped forwards, her hair falling down in curtains hiding her face. She could be smiling, I decide. She isnae, but she could be.

"Just time," she says.

"Well, if yer looking tae kill a few minutes, ye could always winch me and then bugger off again."

"That's not fair." She looks up, and her face is red, her freckles looking like tiny wee burns.

"I didnae think so either." I start hitting my heid with a bit more force now, but it quickly becomes too sore, and I have tae stop. I rest the side ae my heid on the handrail so's I can look at her. I like looking at her. Even though I'm not really acting like I do, I really do. I remember how it felt when she touched me and I really, really do. It's the only thing here I think I enjoyed. Her eyebrows break my fucking heart. "And I still dinnae ken yer name."

"Maybe it's better that ye dinnae ken my name. Ken? I mean, when this is all over, we'll need tae go our separate ways. That might be easier with no labels. Maybe we'll not get hurt this time."

I sit up straight. "Is that what this is about? Because I wouldnae hurt ye. I wouldnae ever hurt ye."

"Ye say that now, but ye dinnae ken."

"I ken what sort of person I am."

"Ye've done it before, Billy," she says.

And that just fucks with my heid, so it does. The joke's on me right enough. The stork watches us. Its gaze switches between the two ae us, like it's waiting for someone tae say something. The lassie, however, seems tae have lost interest and after one last kick at the dirt, she starts tae walk away.

"Where ye going now?" I ask.

She sighs and turns back, maybe only three steps further away than before.

"I need tae go build a cage," she says.

And even though it's a fucking random thing tae say, I still had an idea she was going tae say it, although I dinnae ken I kent until after she'd said it. Fuck it. I ken that disnae make much sense, but as it spins round my heid, I reckon if I can make it spin faster, everything will fall intae place.

"A cage for what?" I ask because I kent I was gonnae ask it.

"A monster," she says, bang on the button, in line with

the script.

"What monster?" I ask, and then I turn the page but the rest ae the scrip isnae there and now I dinnae ken with she's gonnae say and all I have is a wish that I hadn't asked.

"You," she says.

And as she turns and wanders off, and while I let her, I keep in my heid a picture ae her—a picture that I dinnae think happened, or hasnae happened yet—a flash ae her crying, less freckles, a bit aulder. At the same time, the decking starts tae vibrate, and at first, I blame the carpet sweeper, thinking that the vibration's pouring out ae the caravan, but then the ground starts tae vibrate too, and my eyes cannae keep up with it, so it looks like there's half a dozen ae everything. The lassie disnae seem tae feel it. She keeps on walking, and as she's strobing intae the distance, I see that face again, fewer freckles now, a wee beauty spot, a wee Marilyn, with cages for her monsters and I ken she felt that, I ken she does feel it because I remember her thinking it.

"Angela," I say.

3

He refused to be distracted because he was so close. The process of counting down was a simple one— he kept telling himself that—but he suspected the process itself was trying to confuse matters. The process threw spanners in the works, asked questions about starting points, made observations about limits, sounded alarms that were off-pitch and constant and may have always been there, but now had grown louder and almost drowned out the hum. The noise continued to build, continued to grow louder until he vocalised it and then the huda-huda-huda reached a peak and banged and zapped and a surge of energy pulsed through him, clenching everything, tensing it all up. The numbers changed colours as white worms of charge inched among them and formed a flash of equations; countless long complicated equations with the one, identical answer. But he refused to be distracted. He continued to count down towards zero. He was so close. Almost there.

2

chase after her but even though she's not that far ahead ae me, the trembling ground makes it like someone's pulling the carpet out from under my feet. With my arms out for balance, I cannae manage much more than a quick walk for fear ae falling on my arse again.

"Angela," I call out. It feels daft hearing myself say this. There's no reason why I should ken her name but I dinnae need a reason tae ken I'm right. There's nae contentment with this certainty. If anything, it makes everything that wee bitty more abnormal and right now, there's nae shortage ae the bizarre in all ae this. "Angela, hold on."

I reach out, and my fingers wrap around her wrist, twist her back tae me, and then my hand slips intae hers, our fingers interlocked. She faces me, but her eyes are everywhere except looking intae mine. I frown, lean towards her tae get a better look.

"Angela, is that you?"

"Why are ye doing this?" Her voice wobbles as she asks and all ae a sudden she disnae seem like the strong-willed lassie fae earlier when she was happy tae rip the pish out ae me about burying a budgie. Now, she's fragile.

"I'm not doing anything," I say. "What is it I'm doing?"

She tugs at her hand, tries tae get free, but I've got too guid a grip.

"I've dealt with this. I've dealt with you. I dinnae need tae be dealing with it all again, Billy. I dinnae need tae be doing this. I was happy, ye ken?"

"Then what are ye doing winching me if ye cannae stand me?"

She stops struggling and then her thumb is gently stroking my hand, her face breaking intae a humourless smile, her gaze finally finding me. "I've always loved ye in my dreams."

An almighty breeze blows fae the back, and I ken it's the stork landing behind me. I dinnae look, though. I cannae look. I need tae focus on this. This is important. There's something I feel I need tae say before I forget.

"I've missed ye, Angela," I say. The ground bucks and we nearly spill over but it disnae stop me from laughing, and it disnae stop me sobbing. "I've missed ye so much."

And as she looks at me and I see tears well in her eyes that quickly swell and burst and run free, and I start tae remember being fourteen and being here with her and how the source ae everything I ever became narrows tae a pinpoint in this caravan site, tae this moment but at a different time, and me being the awkward wee cunt I used tae be and I still dinnae ken what she ever seen in me apart from a future and even that turned sour.

"I travelled halfway round the world tae get away from ye, Billy," she says, and I begin tae understand my mistake. What I thought was longing in her tears is really anger.

"Angela, I—"

"Halfway round the world tae start a new life. Ye forced me away from my pals, from my family. From my own laddie. Ye made me destroy every relationship I ever had. That was the price I had tae pay, ye see? That's how much it cost tae get away from you."

"What—"

"And it's still not enough. D'ye have any idea what that feels like? Tae ken that ye can still control me and there's nae escape, not even when I'm thousands ae miles away from ye, Billy. Not even when yer fucking deid."

The ground bucks again—a bigger one this time—and then she breaks out from my grip, and everything goes white, and it takes me a wee second tae work out what's going on, and eventually I realise that the white in front ae me isnae flat and it isnae a light, but it has texture. It's feathered, and it's the purest white. It's pristine.

The stork stands between me and Angela, and it's stretched up tae its full height and its beak's open like it's swallowing a fish and it beats its massive wings at the space between us, pushing us further apart. I try tae move round it, but it keeps stepping intae me and then a new vibration starts, over and above the one that's determined tae knock me down. I feel it in my feet and my gut, and I think it's coming from the stork. I think it's screaming at me, but it's hard tae tell because everything else is far too loud. And I'm just one big swinging fist now, desperate tae get by tae my Angela, tae sort things out, my heid flinched back tae avoid they flapping fucking wings, and I feel I brush something with a couple ae blows, and then I connect full, one hundred percent, and as I pull my fist back again for the knockout, all the noise in the world is sucked away and I freeze, and the ice feeds intae me from every pore, pulls intae my core tae form a single, miniscule point and then it evaporates. Once that happens, the ground stops shaking, and the only things I can hear are the stork's wings flapping in my face, someone telling me tae stay calm, and my mam going fucking mental with the carpet sweeper.

Huda-huda-huda. Huda-huda-huda. Huda-huda-huda. Huda-huda-huda. Huda-huda-huda. Huda-huda-huda.

Angela's lying out on the stones that form the big circle round the long grass in the middle ae the caravan site. Curled up intae a ball. Clutching her stomach. Rocking herself. Eyes clenched shut. Teeth bared. A damp patch spread out from the crotch ae her jeans. As it spreads, it gathers, and it runs red across the stones.

—Stay calm.

"Angela," I whisper.

—Stay calm, Billy.

"Angela, hen. Are ye alright? Yer bleeding, sweetheart."

—Billy, you stay fucking calm now, mister. Yer nearly done.

I go tae her, couch down on my hunkers, my hands hovering above her wee body like I'm afraid tae touch her, or that something's stopping me. The smell ae iron rises from her like heat.

—This had tae happen, Billy, but ye need tae be calm. Ye've done so well up tae now.

I snap my heid round in the direction ae the voice. It's just me and the stork. In the distance making their way towards us is my big brother and my wee sister, but they're still too far away.

—Keep calm, Billy, the stork says. It towers above me like I'm a dwarf,

"Billy, is it?" I snap. "We're on first name terms, is that right?"

—If it makes ye happier, my name's Ba.

"Well, Ba, since when could you fucking talk?" I ask.

—I've always been able tae talk. Ye've just never thought tae ask me fuck all tae find out.

My heid's spinning so much I'm scared it's gonnae unscrew itself, but there's something about the stork's voice, now I listen tae it properly, that does calm me down.

"What's wrong with her?" ah ask, standin up.

—Can ye not remember? It's history repeating. She kent it would happen. Right from the start, she kent.

Angela squeezes herself intae a tighter ball, her arms wrapped round her middle, and now her face is so red that the veins are standing out on her neck. There's not a sound coming from her. Not even a whimper.

—Dinnae worry, though. She'll be right as rain after ye fuck off. Well, for now anyway. Yon wee beauty spot ye were always so taken with? Malignant melanoma. She'll be deid inside six months. But that's not for you tae worry yourself about. You'll be long gone before that happens.

"No! Angela!" I try tae go tae her again but they wings really are fucking massive, and the stork pushes me away so easy, I might as well be made ae polystyrene.

—C'mon now, Billy. Calm yerself. Ye've done so well. Dinnae lose it now.

"I need tae help her."

—Billy, man. No matter what ye try tae dae, it's not gonnae change anything. Ye cannae fuck about with history. Ye needed tae help her twelve year ago. Ye didnae. That was when it really would've mattered.

"But...but I'm just fourteen."

—Yer not really getting any ae this, are ye? It's not quite sinking in. She's here because you put her here. She's going through this again because you needed tae see it again. She's that age because you made it that way. Just like ye had her running about like a blue-arsed flea tae get back for yer funeral. Ye almost had her as well, until I stepped in. See, outside yer heid, back in the living and breathing, she didnae even try. D'ye hear me? She didnae even try. Ye needed tae come away with that sentiment if ye wurnae comfy with coming away with the whole thing. She didnae even try, Billy. You keep that in mind. She didnae even try.

"I'm too fucking young tae deal with any ae this."

—Well, that's a pity, because one things for sure, pal; yer not gonnae get any aulder.

I've nae control over anything. That's the first thing I realise. All ae this—all ae it—is happening whether I'm involved or not. Leaving the caravan, digging the hole, seeing the auld guy at the peninsula, I'd've done all that whether I wanted tae or not. Of course, because I thought it was my choice, there's nae real difference. Bottom line, I guess, is that it happened. Even if somebody else had the remote control, even it that somebody else turned out tae be me. And none ae this makes one single fucking ounce ae sense.

—Now, yer getting it, says the stork with a nod. C'mon. It's nearly time. We need tae be wrapping this up, and there's nae show without Punch.

1

The journey back tae the caravan takes much longer than I thought it would. On a level that wasnae quite tangible, I understood why this was the case. Delaying tactics always were a favourite ae mine. I also got the sense—maybe from Ba—that everything was falling back intae place, the stars were moving, shite was aligning. This might all be my own doing, but there's still a protocol. The more I thought about it, the more it seemed far-fetched enough to be true.

Up ahead, somehow overtaking me and Ba, my big brother and wee sister head back tae the caravan and tae my mam who I can see is standing out on the decking, the caravan door open wide, the rainbow-coloured fly blinds blowing round her shoulders like tenticles.

Behind me, I ken Angela has moved on tae wherever it is she needs tae be. I wonder if any ae this will leave even the slightest taste in her mouth, if maybe she'll wake up with a memory ae me in her heid and what she'll do and how she'll feel if that's the case. She'd probably feel betrayed by herself, and for the first time since all ae this started, I feel sad. I feel remorse. I'm sorry.

—Nobody said this was gonnae be easy, Ba says.

"I ken," I say. "It's just that I always imagined dying would be the easiest thing in the world. It'd be like falling off yer bike. But it's not. It's fucking hard, so it is. The hardest thing I'll ever have tae dae."

—The thing about falling off yer bike is, even when ye ken yer going down, ye still try like a bastard tae stay upright. Yer instinct is tae stay on.

"And what the fuck does a stork ken about falling off a bike?"

—Am I wrong?

Up at the caravan, the group's splitting up. My mam and my big brother walk tae the embankment, while my wee sister walks tae me. My mam's left the caravan door open, I notice, and the fly blinds still bellow and dance in a wind that I can see, but cannae feel.

It's not until she's only about twenty feet away from me that I notice my sister's not really walking towards me at all. Her path, which has been pretty much unbroken since she started heading away from the caravan is at more ae an angle and the course we're on means we'll not meet. Then, when she's even closer, I dinnae ken who she is, but she's not my wee sister. She's not Helen either. But I think I might recognise her.

One thing's for sure, she recognises me. She glares at me, pure hate in her eyes and as she gets closer still, I start tae worry that the wee thing's gonnae attack me. But she disnae. In fact, she disnae say a word. But that expression remains fixed on her face until after we pass, less that five feet away from each other.

"That's not my sister," I whisper tae Ba. For some reason, even though I'm getting a better grip on the rules round here, I still dinnae want her tae overhear.

—And you're no fourteen. But these are your thoughts, Billy. Cause and fucking effect. Dae ye even have a sister?

I try tae stop, but Ba's having none ae it and he drags me on so I end up walking backwards so I can watch the lassie I thought was my wee sister crouch down at the spot where Angela was curled up in a ball. And then slowly, she fades like an auld painting and just before she disappears completely and forever, the one thought that jumps intae my heid is how much I like the name Rebecca.

—Yer a guid lassie, Rebecca.

It's not Ba who says this. It's not me who thinks it. I dinnae ken where it comes from. I know it's true.

When we get tae the caravan and the open door, I dinnae even try tae get tae it. Big Ba's in the road for one, but I ken it's not in the plan. I ken where this is leading. I ken where we're going.

Between the caravan and the embankment, there's the hole that I dug with a shovel and with my bare hands and my fingers. There's the hole that's still wet from my sweat. At points, I thought I was just digging tae pass the time. At other points, I thought I was digging something up. It turns out, though, that all that time I was really digging my own grave. If I'd kent that at the start, I'd've made a better fucking job ae it.

Round the hole, waiting, there's the auld fishing guy, my mam and my big brother. Except at some point, the players have been subbed. There's Raymond, Raymond's Helen and my laddie.

"Adam," I say. "My laddie."

He's standing right next tae the hole, his eyes fixed on his shiny black shoes that almost touch the edge. Without moving his heid, he looks at me, but my gaze must be too pleading and too heavy tae hold because he quickly goes back to watching his shoes.

Except for the fact that they're all dead solemn, likes, it's only the auld fishing guy—our Raymond—that actually looks sad.

"Alright, folks," I say.

Nobody answers.

"Can they not hear me?" I say tae Ba.

—These guys? It's best that they cannae. Not now.

"Can I not hear them?"

—That wouldnae really be fair, would it?

"What happened tae my real mam? Where's she? Is she already deid?"

—I fucking hope so. Ye buried her.

So the three ae them stand there, round this hole in the ground and that's all there is now. There's nae embankment, nae caravan, nae vegetable patch, nae circle ae stones, nae peninsula, nae wee stream that's not deep enough for skimmers. There's just the three ae them, a minister that I dinnae recognise and me and my big stork pal. The minister disnae have any books or notes, but he's chattering away guid style. I cannae hear him neither.

And then the enormity ae where I am and what's about tae happen hits me, and the thought that screams out when I watch this scene unfold is that I didnae want tae get buried. I didnae want tae be stuffed in a box or trapped like a bit ae jewellery. I didnae want worms nibbling on my toes for all eternity. I wanted tae get burnt. I wanted tae get thrown tae the winds, and I wanted my ashes tae travel far and wide, tae places I'd only dreamt ae.

"Tae Egypt," I says tae Ba because I ken he'd be reading my thoughts. "I always was fascinated by Egypt. But the only person I told any ae this tae was Angela, and that's nae fucking use tae naebody."

The longer it goes on, the more separated I feel from the group. Ba kens what the minister's saying. I ken he does, but he's not for telling me. I don't suppose he's saying anything earth-shattering, nothing that'll make any difference. Still. It'd be nice tae ken.

When the minister's done, I see him smile and hold out his hands, inviting the others tae have a word or two. Raymond shakes his heid. He never was one for big speeches, and he just looks at the sky and sighs. Then he picks up some earth and lobs it intae the hole.

Huda-huda-huda.

Everything shudders.

Helen's next. She was like a sister tae me. Then she was like a maid. I let that happen. I did fuck all tae stop it. I ken she's got plenty tae say for herself and plenty tae get off her chest, but in the end, she says only five words and I dinnae even think she says them loud enough for anyone else tae hear. Ba hears it, and he disnae contradict me when I think the words myself.

—Nothing was ever guid enough.

She picks up a handful ae dirt and drops it intae the hole.

Huda-huda-huda.

Another wee tremor accompanies that one.

Last, there's my laddie. He's a journalist, ye ken. He's got himself a nice lassie. I've never heard her talk so I dinnae ken what she'd have tae say about any ae this but from what I've seen, she's a braw wee thing, so she is. She's not here because there's a wee baby on the way. It burns me a little tae ken that I'll not see the bairn, but there'd always be something, I suppose. First words, first steps, first day at school. It's never a guid time. I miss my laddie, and for every day he made me proud, I'm sure I was nothing more than a fucking disappointment tae him. Those two dinnae cancel each other out. They repel. They push further apart.

There's a million things coursing round his heid. For some reason, he's sorry.

He reaches intae his inside pocket and pulls out my wee stork ornament. He holds on tae it for a second, close tae his heart. Then he brings it tae his mouth, and he whispers something tae it; a secret between him and me; a thought tae keep me warm, and then he lets it go. He wanted tae love me.

Huda-huda-huda. Huda-huda-huda. Huda-huda-huda.

And now there's a bigger tremble, a vibration that I ken isnae gonnae stop. The ground crumbles, and very quickly it becomes very out ae control until it's deafening and everything slides and it's only gonnae get worse.

—Come on in, number five, shouts Ba. Yer time is up.

"There's no going back now."

—Got it in one.

And his wing wraps round me, and he flings me ontae his back as the wee circle ae dirt crumbles and collapses, and the people drop away, back tae wherever they need tae be, and it feels like me and Ba are soaring but we might be plummeting, and it disnae really matter one way or the other because the stars are washing in and out, like they're caught in a current, and it's hard tae care too much about anything when what ye've got right at that minute is so beautiful and complete. I've got a guid hold ae Ba's neck and I ken he's not gonnae let me off until we get tae where we need tae be going because that's his job.

I dinnae ken if it's the sensation ae being with the stars or where the feeling really comes from, but I try tae make a promise that if I get another shot at this, I'll do better. I'll try harder. I'll be a better person. But even before the thought's properly finished forming in my heid, I realise the folly ae making promises like that. Ah mean, it's not as if we ever make resolutions tae be bastards and bampots. Some ae us just turn out that way. We've nae control over any ae that shite and if there's one thing I've learnt through all ae this, it's this simple truth; undeniable, constant, singular, universal, perhaps the simplest ae all:

Folk are fannies, and they fuck things up.

0

In his mind, there lived a picture of a house and that house had doors. Beyond the doors were people and inside the people were memories of every joke they'd ever heard, every occasion they'd ever celebrated, every embrace they'd ever shared, every point they'd ever argued, every promise they'd ever broken and every mistake they'd ever made. Many of these memories were common between the people and for anyone looking in, it was like the memories actually belonged to the house. For a while, the house was a happy one and although other emotions came in and washed over the memories from time to time, they never fully covered the happiness. Happiness was a constant. Happiness was what held everything together. But then the house became so unhappy, people forgot the happy memories had ever existed and the deeper the unhappiness became rooted, the more it consumed everything until some people found a way out and escaped and took their memories with them. Eventually, even the last remaining person had to leave, and as they left, their final thought was a knowledge that they would never come back. For a while, even though there were no people in the house, some of the old memories had clung on. They grabbed on to the furniture, seeped into the walls and the curtains, dripped from the ceiling down through the walls to the floor, soaked through the papers and keepsakes, into tables and chairs and old photographs and for as long as they lasted, they were painful memories because they knew they should've escaped with the others and now it was like they were being torn from their natural habitat, separated from their loved ones, ripped from protective arms to keep an empty house warm. In time, though, they too faded, and then the picture began to disappear because it didn't have a reason to remain any longer. But in the background, there's a hum, and like any other hum, it's not always easy to tell where it's coming from or how loud it is and eventually, he becomes so used to the hum that he doesn't even notice it's there until the time comes when he needs to hear it, to remember what it sounds like and once he tunes in to it, he recognises it like an old friend and he smiles because while he will never follow it, it's good to feel that it's there and it will forever know the way back home.

ACKNOWLEDGEMENTS

In the summer of 2010, I wrote the first draft of this book. It took seven weeks. In the following years, I've been blessed to be surrounded by people who have helped me make it better. These people include Julie Dunion, Daphne Hamilton, Karen Jones, Sam Robinson, Eileen McMurdo, Angie Campbell, Steve Fitzpatrick, Stephen Higham, Meg Higham, the good people at Alloa Writers, Stirling Writers Group, Eaton Rapids Writers Group and the online workshops at Chapter 79, Scrawl, and Writers Dock. To these people, and those I've forgotten, my heartfelt thanks. Particular thanks and love go to my wife and my champion, Helen Broom, for her help and belief and whose persistence is the reason this book exists anywhere other than a hard drive. Cheers, m'darlin.

Gavin Broom
Eaton Rapids, Michigan
October 2018

NOTE FROM THE PUBLISHER

We hope you have enjoyed *The Scottish Book of the Dead* by Gavin Broom. The greatest compliment you can give to the author is to leave an on-line review of the book on the site where you made your purchase.

This novel contains many non-American spelling variants; however if you observe spelling or grammar errors that go beyond the Scottish dialect and United Kingdom spelling, we'd be happy to know about these. Please contact us at islandcitypublishing@gmail.com.

ABOUT THE AUTHOR

Born in Falkirk, Scotland in 1973, Gavin Broom moved to Eaton Rapids, Michigan in the summer of 2012 where he currently lives with his wife, Helen, and three stepchildren, Nick, Benen, and Estella. Over the years, he's had over seventy short stories and poems published online and in print, and his collection, *A Documentary About Sharks*, is available on Amazon.

The Scottish Book of the Dead is his debut novel and is a hugely personal work, dealing as it does with his own inability to handle grief. His beloved grandfather passed away in 1990, followed by his father eight years later, and it wasn't until after he finished the book that he realized how his experiences inspired many of the events, and how he had disassociated himself from these emotions, refusing to acknowledge that they existed. He's getting better. Slowly.

Gavin has made a home for himself and his family in Michigan, but there are still occasional longings from across the Atlantic, whispers from a previous life. Particularly, the wind that would carry over the Ochil Hills, across the fields to the Coffee Bothy where a mean bowl of lentil soup and fabulous scone would be served, long summer nights where the sun never seemed to set for long, proper fish and chips, rolls on square sausage, Tennent's Lager, and of course, family and friends. And a house, where happy memories will always outnumber the bad.

37945995R00134

Printed in Great Britain
by Amazon